# A Shamrock in the Snow

*The story of a Canadian hero*
**Thomas D'Arcy McGee**

# *A Shamrock in the Snow*

*The story of a Canadian hero*
*Thomas D'Arcy McGee*

An historical novel
by

**MICHAEL LEO DONOVAN**

Published by
Jesperson Publishing Limited

Copyright © 1996 Michael Leo Donovan

All rights reserved. No part of this publication may be reproduced or transmitted in any form or by any means without written permission of the publisher.

**Jesperson Publishing Limited**
39 James Lane
St. John's, NF Canada
A1E 3H3

*Cover and Book Design:* Donna Snelgrove
*Printing and Binding:* Jesperson Press Limited
*Back Cover Picture (Michael Donovan):* Jane Butler

Jesperson Publishing acknowledges the financial support of the *Canada Council* towards its publishing program.

The publisher acknowledges a financial contribution from the *Cultural Affairs Division* of the *Department of Culture, Recreation and Youth* of the Government of Newfoundland and Labrador which has helped make this publication possible.

Printed in Canada.

**Canadian Cataloguing in Publication Data**

Donovan, Michael Leo, 1954-

    A shamrock in the snow

    ISBN 0-921692-74-9

1. McGee, Thomas D'Arcy, 1825-1868 - - Fiction.  I. Title

PS8557.066S42  1996        C813'.54        C96-950042-4
PR9199.3.D66S42  1996

*To my parents, whose lives were my first storybooks; Halina, who always believed, and Leo, who knew a good idea when he came up with this one.*

# Acknowledgement

With thanks to Stewart Harding for his patience and counsel.

*Thomas D'Arcy McGee*

# Prologue

## *Ottawa*
## *April 7, 1868*

Roses were blooming as near as Hamilton, but it was a cold Canadian night in Ottawa, with much winter snow still on the ground. A well-dressed forty-three-year-old man turned up gas-lit Sparks Street, and headed toward the house he lived in. Hearing the scuffling of footsteps behind him, he stopped, and turned.

"Who goes there?"

His breath escaped in tiny ghosts. He heard nothing. The man shrugged, then turned up the stairs of his official residence. He stopped at the front door, foraged around in his coat pocket, and produced a key. It was when he worked the key into the door that the ghost of someone else's cold breath suddenly wafted up against his face. It froze him.

A gun went off, a loud BANG, and the well-dressed man collapsed to the icy pavement. The muffled footfalls of the unidentified assassin ran off into the night. The fallen man whispered through a final cloud of frosty breath... "James, what have you done to us?"

Then a shrill, frightened voice rang out, "He's been shot! D'Arcy McGee's been shot!"

The Father of Confederation closed his eyes as thick drops of blood blossomed like roses in the white snow around his head.

# Chapter One

*Carlingford, County Louth, Ireland
The Summer of 1831*

Two mischievous young boys ran from their mother and into the forgiving arms of a field of green. D'Arcy, the elder, led the way. James lost his brother quickly in the grass that towered over them. Neither could tell that armies had trampled these fields many times for centuries, because always the countryside had healed itself. Always the green grew back.

D'Arcy could tell you why, if you asked him, because his father had once explained it to him. He'd said that when God cried, His tears fell on Ireland. And that was also why, D'Arcy would sputter with wide-eyed earnestness, that this was where the shamrocks grew.

The running D'Arcy and James collided somewhere in the middle of this field soothed by God's tears and sated on Irish blood. They tumbled over each other with laughter. Then D'Arcy, older but no larger than his brother, lifted James onto his tiny shoulders. James still couldn't see his mother, but he gasped at the vast sea of green. It went on as far as his wide eyes could see. But truth be told, no Irishman could see beyond Ireland.

"See her?" came the struggling voice beneath him. But before James could answer, a velvet-fisted voice punched out at them.

"D'Arcy! James! You boys come back here!"

The sound knocked James from D'Arcy's shoulders.

It was then, while crouched down in hiding and struggling to keep from laughing, that the six-year-old D'Arcy noticed something at his feet.

A gun.

A large gun by his tiny feet. He lifted the rotted wood and rusted metal piece by its barrel, and studied it as he would some strange, exotic animal. Then he tossed it aside. Finding his mother's voice more interesting, more magnetic, he leapt up, and bounded through the grass toward her, squealing with prankish laughter.

Seeing him, she shook her head and teased with enormous affection, "Thomas D'Arcy McGee, what will become of you?" His eyes squeezed shut to make room in his expression for a huge grin. She studied her son's unhandsome little face and his unruly mass of black hair, and her heart swelled.

Then, as she gathered him in her generous arms, "I thought I asked you to look after your brother." With that she looked past him, and her warm expression became one of sudden terror.

Four-year-old James had found the discarded pistol and was waving it above his head. He was laughing joyously.

## Dublin 1846

"D'Arcy!"

A man's voice rang out on the busy Dublin street, and a twenty-one-year-old man turned around. The years had not performed miracles on D'Arcy McGee's looks; his hair was still unmanageable and his face plain and forgettable.

But he was already more than a confident man with eyes black as a starless night and a quick, disarming smile. The maturing D'Arcy was a man of energy and enthusiasm, a tangle of wit and wisdom. His irrepressible charm was reflected in the faces of those who addressed him.

On this early morning those faces belonged to Charles Gavan Duffy, the publisher of *The Nation*, a Catholic newspaper working toward the peaceful re-unification and freedom of Ireland, and John Mitchel, the editor. D'Arcy wrote for the same paper, and the men were obviously happy together, idealistic in their cause. As they walked along the street they talked with conviction about the new flag for THEIR Ireland. It would be tri-coloured: green for Catholic Ireland, orange for Protestant Ireland, and white for the peace that would exist between them in a free country.

Then Mitchel grabbed the diminutive D'Arcy by the back of his coat and shook him good-naturedly, "The Irish people have been held down for so long, they almost accept this lowly position as their proper place—and educating them differently will probably take seventy years. What do you say to that, my enthusiastic young friend?"

"What would I say?" D'Arcy pulled himself away from the doubting Mitchel, straightened his clothing, "Only that, at that slow pace I guess I'll be the only one left of us to see it."

The other two men looked at each other. Then Duffy said, "He's got you there, Mitchel."

"Speak for yourself, you bloody old goat."

They arrived at *The Nation's* front door in a wave of laughter, and Mitchel offered a drink from his flask. The others turned it down, but Mitchel drank deeply. Then he grinned, "God gave the Irish whiskey to keep them from taking over the world."

D'Arcy, Duffy and Mitchel stepped inside the two-storey building to find it in a controlled confusion. News had arrived at dawn that the police were coming to question and detain the whole *Nation* editorial staff because of some alleged anti-British commentary in their last issue.

"Bloody harassment!" Duffy bellowed.

The police had practised this form of interference before. The meddling was an attempt to keep the staff from getting the paper out on time. But a solution had already been arrived at— *The Nation* would still be published because a group of wives and girlfriends and sympathizers were already arriving to do the work! A parade of women took their positions along the press as the regular male staff scrambled out the door.

D'Arcy grabbed one worker as he slipped past and asked where the tip-off came from. But the answer itself stepped out behind him.

"Where would you be without your brother?" grinned the younger McGee through an unwashed face.

James at nineteen was much less accomplished than his brother. He was simple, sweet, and overly helpful—though his edges were a little rougher. But even his scruffy demeanour and hand-me-down clothing couldn't hide his roguish good looks. D'Arcy was everything his brother wasn't. James' only coin was handsome.

D'Arcy was happy to see him, and grateful for the warning.

"Where've you been, lad?"

"What you don't know won't hurt me," James grinned.

When D'Arcy asked James how he came upon the information, James just shrugged, "You know me D'Arcy—

always hanging around with the wrong people."

Just then publisher Duffy appeared at James' side, "Your brother tells me that you're looking for work."

James glanced at D'Arcy, and shuffled with some discomfort, "Yeah. Sure." What nineteen-year-old wasn't?

"Well, I can use all the quick-witted McGees I can get."

Embarrassed, James clutched at the coat-tail of his jacket. D'Arcy's old jacket. "Thank you, Mr. Duffy."

"You can thank your brother."

James looked over at his brother, but D'Arcy's attention had drifted across the room. He'd caught sight of a very beautiful young lady.

"Let's go!" yelled Duffy as he grabbed his young writer, but D'Arcy kept looking back.

"Who's that?" he asked.

The publisher followed D'Arcy's pin-pointed stare, and chuckled, "That's Mary Cafferty, young D'Arcy."

D'Arcy grinned with appreciation, "She's stolen my heart."

"Petty larceny, at best," quipped the publisher as the men ran out into the streets.

His name was Daniel O'Connell, and his followers were legion. He was the father of the movement that embraced the hopes and feverish dreams of the young men and women of this battered Ireland. And on this sunny afternoon spread out on the Irish countryside, his every eloquent word was being digested in a feeding frenzy by a huge crowd. O'Connell and his speech sang the praises of a 'peaceful' negotiation with England, a concept that presumed the Irish capable of such a thing. England's propaganda had made the world believe otherwise.

O'Connell didn't need to be told that British soldiers were on the horizon, keeping a watchful eye over the proceedings. In fact, they followed him from town to town like a private security force, but their intentions were less comforting to the charismatic leader. Their purpose was to dampen the spirits of the movement's followers, and with their own blood if the opportunity presented itself.

D'Arcy and Mitchel watched with concern as O'Connell, not wanting any trouble, decided to cut his speech short. The crowd's enthusiasm threatened to turn ugly, but O'Connell deftly handled and redirected their energy. He was a master, and D'Arcy was impressed. But Mitchel was disenchanted.

"What the hell is he so afraid of?"

"He's afraid OF nothing," said D'Arcy in the man's defence, "he's afraid FOR us."

"Malarkey!" Mitchel spat. "We can take care of ourselves."

"It wouldn't matter. The British would tell the world that we started it, and deserved the consequences."

The crowd began to disperse, and D'Arcy and his editor started toward their horse-drawn carriage. As they did, James stepped in behind them, listening to the argument with bemusement, seemingly without opinion one way or another.

After a deep swig from his ever-ready flask, Mitchel erupted, "The time for non-violent dealings with England is over. Everyone's too comfortable with the way things are," he said. "Change will only come about now with force. Besides," he argued, "England has painted an international picture of the Irish as uneducated, drunken animals—let's live up to it!" His last words were drowned in a mouthful of whiskey.

"Live down to it, you mean." D'Arcy countered. "I'm not so anxious to prove the British right on anything."

O'Connell had ended his speech by announcing a massive peaceful demonstration six months down the road, and the crowd's response had been very supportive. D'Arcy suggested his editor wait and see what would happen after the world recognized that Ireland was capable of articulating its unhappiness non-violently.

"Earning the world's sympathy rather than its fear and disgust may bring international pressure to bear on the British," he said with that smile.

"Too little too late," Mitchel shot back. "O'Connell's already proven he's not the man to do it."

Stupefied, D'Arcy just looked at his editor, then laughed, "Where were you when God was handing out patience, Mitchel—slapping babies?"

Someone else laughed, a sound like music to D'Arcy's ears. He turned. The eavesdropper was none other than Mary Cafferty, the woman with D'Arcy's heart.

D'Arcy removed his hat, gestured to their surroundings, and said with some flirtation, "You like to live dangerously, Miss Cafferty."

She smiled a VERY dangerous smile, "You look like a brave man, Mr. McGee."

D'Arcy, floored, glanced at his brother James, who flexed an eyebrow with appreciation. D'Arcy turned again to the young woman, "Can we offer you a lift back, Miss Cafferty?"

Mary accepted, and D'Arcy helped her up and into the coach. When Mitchel and James moved to follow, D'Arcy stopped them in a hushed, humorous tone, "I think this would be a wonderful opportunity for you to air out those ideas of yours, Mitchel. I'm sure my brother will hang on to every word."

Confused, James stuttered, "You're...you're not suggesting that we walk back to *The Nation*, are you?"

Before Mitchel could add his voice to the discordant chorus, D'Arcy took him into his confidence with a wink, "Mitchel, is it possible that my own flesh and blood is this significantly out of charm's way?" Then the young writer gestured into the carriage at Mary.

Taken aback, Mitchel looked at James, who smiled awkwardly.

D'Arcy patted his editor on the shoulder and wagged a finger at his brother, "Now you keep your mouth shut, dear brother. We have much to learn from the worldly John Mitchel."

"And plenty of time to learn it," added Mitchel, shaking his head.

So, as the carriage carrying D'Arcy and Mary started off, so did Mitchel with young James. The different paths taken on this day would influence the McGee brothers for a lifetime.

It would also influence history.


Soon, Mitchel and James had walked well beyond the crowds, where the scenery was spectacular.

"You don't say much, do you James?"

"I let my hands do the talking," he said quickly, lifting his clenched hands in emphasis. Then, rethinking this crudeness with his new employer, he stuck his hands into his pockets and added, "Besides, D'Arcy has enough to say for the both of us."

Mitchel smiled, but a different set of lines, almost sinister, now creased his face, "Just make sure he's not the only one thinking, young James."

The younger man stared at Mitchel, too humiliated to speak.

So Mitchel went on.

"Your brother is a dreamer." He spat the word like a bad taste out of his mouth, then wiped it with the back of his hand. "Electing sympathetic members to parliament—what's he thinking?" The editor looked at James for an answer, knowing the young man would be too intimidated to offer one. "You and I both know it'll take decades before any good reaches the people of Ireland."

He put his arm around James suddenly, startling him into his confidence, "We have no hope but for a violent revolution against British and class rule. And support is mounting."

James looked at the older man, his face clenched in confusion and curiosity, "Support? What kind of support?"

Mitchel's voice had become a whisper. But it still screamed into the young man's head.

"Today there are men willing to die for Ireland, James."

"Who...who are these people?" Even to James his own voice sounded small, distant.

Insignificant.

"Brave men, James," said Mitchel in a voice so confident it couldn't be wrong. "Irishmen who know in their hearts that if they're not part of this revolution, they're part of nothing at all."

For reasons James couldn't quite understand, his face flushed and his chest swelled.

The carriage manoeuvred over the dirt road. Inside, Mary bounced against the side panel. D'Arcy reached to steady her, but she smartly straightened herself.

"Are you all right?"

"I'm fine, thank you."

"The ride can be rough. People who've never ridden in a carriage often assume—"

"I've been in a carriage before, Mr. McGee."

"Of course, I didn't mean to insinuate—"

He stopped. She was smiling at him. He smiled, and battled not to feel uncomfortable around himself. He looked out at the passing countryside, then back at her. She was still smiling at him, and this time he couldn't tear his eyes away.

"You were saying?"

"Was I?" his voice was soft and warm. For reasons he couldn't quite understand, his face flushed and his chest swelled.

The couple sat in rich, comfortable silence for a long time. Long enough that the carriage had rolled off the carpets of green field, through forests thicker than pipe smoke, and out finally into a huge clearing cluttered with tragedy. In an instant they'd slipped from the Irish dream into the Irish nightmare.

Here, quarter acre plots containing mud-wall cabins with no windows and no chimney were home to desperately poor peasant families. Mary's eyes fell on one particular clan, six children and a pig crammed into a one room shack. They were all on their knees now trying to save a humble patch of potato crop, much of it rotted black.

"The potato famine has begun eating the Irish people," hissed D'Arcy through clenched teeth.

Suddenly, six British soldiers on horseback appeared out of nowhere, sweeping down the gentle slope toward the labouring family. The frightened children fell over each other trying to find a place to hide.

There was none.

"What are they doing? What do they want with those poor people?"

"Security check," D'Arcy sighed with sarcasm, "as if those poor bastards are capable of anything more than the fight to stay alive."

Mary caught her breath as a soldier grabbed hold of an old man, pulled him up from his knees, then threw him back down, crushing his delicate labours.

"Mr. McGee—!" she blurted, then covered her mouth.

D'Arcy looked at her, back at the scene below, then leaned out the carriage window.

"Driver! Stop, will you."

D'Arcy and Mary walked down the gentle slope. One soldier noticed the well-dressed couple and took a step toward them, but D'Arcy froze him with a look. Then the Officer-in-Charge glanced at the approaching party, and called his men out from the small shack. They joined the others and galloped away, their bright, clean and colourful uniforms in stark contrast to the peasants left behind, still rooted in poverty.

A child, just several degrees away from nakedness, was the only one not frightened by D'Arcy's presence. The young writer bent to one knee and handed the tiny, filthy waif a coin.

"What's your name, colleen?"

There came a tiny voice from behind the dirt, "Deirdre." Then she smiled, holding out a bundle of rags with a string tied tight round its middle, "And this is Maureen."

"I believe you two are the prettiest little girls I've ever seen." She smiled more broadly, and wiped her wet nose.

Just then one brother broke away from the potato crop, a child himself, and pulled his sister roughly away. As he did, he shouted at the strangers, "We don't care for Protestants around here!"

Mary moved to correct the brave, blustery boy but D'Arcy, startled, asked, "Are you saying you wouldn't take a man's money if he were a Protestant?"

The boy, with hatred in his eyes, said, "I would. But I'd kill him for it." Then the boy dragged his confused sibling back into the tiny room that was their home.

As D'Arcy and Mary turned away he ran a hand through his curly hair, "What do you say to something like that?"

"I know what John Mitchel would say," offered Mary sharply, stopping D'Arcy in his tracks.

"And what's that?"

She lowered her voice into Mitchel's range and stained it with a little alcohol, "This is the by-product of oppressive British rule. How many more generations of these innocents must be sacrificed before your idea of a peaceful settlement comes to pass?"

D'Arcy had no answer, only a deeply troubled expression. Then, her voice changed, and like a soft hand reached out to stroke him, "But John Mitchel chooses not to believe in you, Mr. McGee."

He had turned to walk away, but stopped to face her once more. "Do you believe in me, Mary Cafferty?"

Again she took hold of him with her eyes, and he was at her mercy.

# CHAPTER TWO

"I DO," SAID MARY.

Mary was in a wedding gown she'd sewn herself from countless yards of Irish silk. D'Arcy was in his tailored best.

The priest announced in solemn, deeply religious tones, "Then I now pronounce you man and wife." D'Arcy pulled the veil back over her beautiful face, and gently kissed her. It was the sweetest moment of his short life, and before it was over his face was streaked with tears. And it seemed that a thousand lit church candles fought for a place in every drop.

A huge joyous howl rang out.

The whoop was James McGee's as he grabbed a startled young woman and began to jig with her. This was D'Arcy and Mary's wedding reception, out on the huge property of publisher Gavan Duffy, out in the brilliant afternoon sun. A couple of fiddlers had dozens of guests dancing on the expansive lawn.

D'Arcy and Mary suddenly parted the crowd. Possessed by an unadulterated happiness, he began to dance with the energy of a young buck. Mary was gorgeous, playful and sexy—the perfect foil for his royal jester. The crowd erupted in applause as the two finished their frenzied dance, and then collapsed into each other.

Duffy approached with a drink, and the McGees thanked him profusely for the lend of the land.

"Well," smiled the host, "I feel somewhat responsible for this. You met over my printing press, after all."

"And I suspect we will again," said D'Arcy with a tinge of the inevitable in his voice, and Mary looked at him with concern.

Then her face was overwhelmed by a wicked, prankish grin, "Gentlemen, we have the rest of our lives to deal with the troubles. If I can't distract my husband on my wedding day—"

"Say no more, Mrs. McGee." Duffy grinned, and pushed D'Arcy off toward the dance. He grabbed his wife and leapt back onto the grass.

Suddenly, drunken shouts brought the fiddling to a stop. D'Arcy and Mary turned just as editor John Mitchel stumbled toward them, bellowing... "Where's Duffy?"

The kindly publisher and host made his way over immediately, protective of his celebratory event, "What the hell kind of behaviour is this on McGee's wedding day?"

"O'Connell has backed down," Mitchel spat.

Duffy was shocked, "What?" D'Arcy and Mary quickly came to his side.

Mitchel sat heavily into a chair, tired and drunk. He groaned, his anger boiling just below the surface, "O'Connell was pressured by the British authorities into cancelling his peaceful demonstration." The silence between his statements had become deafening, and people stared in shock. "They convinced him that such a thing was impossible because trouble was all that could come from a gathering of Irish."

D'Arcy glanced at Duffy, but *The Nation's* publisher, in his disappointment, could only look away.

"Where does that leave your movement now?" Mitchel challenged the gathering. "Your beloved leader can even be talked out of doing nothing!" Furious, Mitchel stood, then stepped toward Duffy, "How about you and your paper, Duffy? You finally prepared to do something?"

"You've left me no alternative," Duffy said in a tired voice, then put his hand on Mitchel's shoulder, "you're fired, John."

Everyone was startled, no one more than *The Nation's* former editor. After staring at his old boss for a difficult moment, Mitchel turned and stumbled away.

D'Arcy, frightened and confused, watched him go.

Mary knew the depth of this tragedy for D'Arcy without having to look at his face. But she did, and knew she had to do something quickly. It would look to those who would remember that she was trying to save her wedding. But the truth was that for the first of what would be many times, she moved to protect her new husband.

She snatched D'Arcy's hand, turned to the fiddlers, and announced in a loud, proud voice, "Gentlemen, for my wedding the Good Lord gave me a sunny day and the handsomest man in all of Ireland. I'm going to dance—with you or without you!"

One instrument at a time the music began anew, and before the day was gone, Mary had made certain that all her friends and family had been to nothing less than an Irish wedding.

The sun disappeared for three days and nights. But D'Arcy did not spend this time struggling with the fit of his two new outfits—that of husband and that of editor. It would have been in vain, because the love he had for Mary, and the ideas he had for *The Nation* both, had broader shoulders than he. So instead, he and his new bride leapt into the busy streets and dirt paths of Ireland, in search of a voice. A voice worth listening to. A voice worthy of a newspaper's headlines. It would have to rise strong and clear from the ground-up dust of crushed spirits and broken hearts, and with a bold new vision from eyes stung by the airborne dust of shattered dreams. It was on the morning of the fourth day that D'Arcy returned to work with the new found voice of *The Nation*.

As he paced around the press, mumbling aloud the ideas germinating inside his head, brother James removed a sign hanging over an office door which read EDITOR JOHN MITCHEL, and replaced it with another reading EDITOR THOMAS D'ARCY McGEE. As he pounded nails into the new wood, D'Arcy stormed past him and sat behind his desk. James watched as D'Arcy began writing his first editorial. His pen flicked and scratched with such intensity, James expected to see the paper spark into flame.

D'Arcy, biting into his tongue as he wrote, read aloud the piece as it spilled out from his conscience and onto the parchment paper, shouting bits and hissing pieces for emphasis as he went. James was startled by the sound of his brother's voice.

> "*In July, 1846, Young Ireland seceded from Daniel O'Connell's peaceful Repeal Association on the object of the lawlessness of shedding blood to achieve political rights. Until then, O'Connell was the absolute ruler of the Irish heart. The old honoured him for his cautious tactics, agreeing that no amount of liberty was worth the spilling of one drop of human blood; the young because England feared and hated him.*"

As he wrote, powerful images illustrating the new and very real horrors of D'Arcy's Ireland slammed against the inside walls of his mind, fragmenting, fuelling the fire in his words. The tiny world of *The Nation's* office disappeared as he saw the poor Irish family being harassed by the British Army. The little ragamuffin Dierdre at his feet—grinning sweetly through the dirt on her face. And he wrote...

*"I cannot endure this state of society any longer. My heart is sick at daily scenes of misery!"*

James stared at his brother now, confused and open-mouthed. Because he couldn't see D'Arcy's thoughts. He couldn't see Mary sitting in the humble McGee home, sewing a little girl's dress.

*"Nothing green, nothing noble will grow in it!"*

Perhaps James couldn't even imagine Mary and D'Arcy as they stood in front of the peasant's shack again, now abandoned. He couldn't see the single grave, or Dierdre's name carved into the humble wood cross. She was four, and would never know what it was like to be five years old.

*"The towns have become one universal poorhouse—the country, one great graveyard!"*

D'Arcy began to sob. Duffy joined James at the door. The men exchanged concerned glances as D'Arcy stabbed his quill back into the inkwell, knocking it askew, his eyes blinded by the memory of his wife as she placed the dress, sewn from a piece torn from her own wedding gown, across Dierdre's grave.

*"The survivors flee to America, with disease festering in their blood."*

D'Arcy tried to blink back the images of poor, exhausted Irish citizens lined up to buy their tickets to America, Australia, and Canada—anywhere but here. He held his head, remembering one woman fainting into her husband's arms.

*"They will lose sight of Ireland on ships that have become floating coffins, carrying them not to America—but eternity. And yet the extermination of the Irish people is not to be apprehended; they cling to the soil like grass, and while they cling, they hate England."*

D'Arcy finally looked up from his work and out from his thoughts and noticed the half-dozen staff members gathered at his door. He grinned suddenly, surprisingly self-satisfied. Then he dipped his quill into the spilled ink one final time, and scrawled with flourish—

*"Signed, Thomas D'Arcy McGee, Editor of* The Nation, *and traitor to the British Government."*

Then he stood, put on his coat, and handed Duffy the editorial on his way out.

"D'Arcy," the weary publisher said, "we can't print this."

"Then find yourself a new Editor."

One of the first to read the new editor's inflammatory headline was the local British commander, and he responded by ordering his soldiers into immediate action.

They invaded *The Nation's* office, damaging the press and recovering as many of the latest issues as possible. They built a mountain of newspapers out on the street, then set them on fire. As day turned into night soldiers continued to feed the fire with more and more copies.

Hours after the soldiers had left, darkness lent itself to the tragedy. Crowds had gathered in silent vigil. The flames continued to turn D'Arcy's words into smoke, and the smoke seemed to make its way into everyone's eyes. But even that couldn't keep Gavan Duffy from staring. D'Arcy looked at his publisher, but found the man's expression unreadable.

"Treat a man like an animal long enough, and he starts thinking like one." D'Arcy turned at the sound of the voice to see his brother step out of the shadows. James was drunk on whiskey and frustration.

"James?" D'Arcy was worried. He'd never seen his brother like this. "Stay with Mary and me tonight, James." He reached out, but his brother pulled away. Then D'Arcy watched helplessly as he ran off into the night.

He knew it was fruitless to call out. He only whispered to himself, "James...what's happening to us?"

A new edition of *The Nation* was necessary, and the staff intended to regroup that very night. D'Arcy was standing in front of a small mirror, shaving his face by candlelight. There was soapy lather in a bowl, and a very sharp straight razor.

He drew the blade across his cheek when Mary entered suddenly, "James has been arrested, D'Arcy. Drunk and disorderly. The British have him."

He reacted almost imperceptively... "I'll have to go get him, Mary." Obviously concerned for the safety of both brothers, she nodded and turned away.

He didn't notice he'd cut his face until he turned his head. Blood had already streaked the white lather on his face, and begun dripping into the soapy bowl below.

D'Arcy stepped up to a soldier guarding the entrance to the British Army Building. The soldier looked at him with a mixture of frustration and disgust, like the Irishman was something he'd tried to throw away before with no success. "I'm here to pick up my brother."

Suddenly recognizing the young writer, the soldier looked

D'Arcy up and down with renewed disgust, then pointed to the building's rear, "He's out back with the pigs, where he belongs."

Indeed, D'Arcy found James outside, cowering in a pen, surrounded with grunting pigs. He couldn't quite make him out in the dark, filthy corner.

"James? James, it's D'Arcy."

"No more," came a pitiful plea. "I beg of you."

"James! I'm here for you, lad! It's D'Arcy!"

Barely a whimper, "D'Arcy." James had begun to cry.

He moved out of the shadows, and D'Arcy could hardly contain his shock. His nineteen-year-old brother had been beaten into a bloody pulp.

D'Arcy began screaming with horror at the sight. Soldiers appeared suddenly out of nowhere, grabbed him roughly and made promises of the same treatment if he didn't keep quiet—about everything.

"Get him out of here!" joked one soldier. "The pigs have been complaining about the smell." Other soldiers laughed.

D'Arcy gathered his barely conscious brother into his arms, and the two moved slowly out of the pen. A soldier spat at D'Arcy as he passed, and his pals laughed again.

"This is what yer brother gets trying to move the British Army out of Ireland all by himself."

James, trying to look up at his brother, winked with pain through a swollen eye, and whispered, "Almost had 'em, too, D'Arcy."

"Shut your bloody mouth, James," D'Arcy hissed fearfully, just as his young brother passed out in his arms.

Mary met them at the door, and helped D'Arcy carry James inside. Once in the candlelight she could make out his face.

"Good lord, D'Arcy!"

"His wounds need cleaning."

Mary covered her mouth, and for a moment she thought she was going to be sick. She turned her head away from James, "How can a man look like that and still be alive?"

D'Arcy placed his brother onto their bed, and then reached to hold her. Then he turned to leave.

"Where are you going?"

"Don't answer the door, and tell no one he's here, will you Mary?"

She stared at him, and for the first time in their young romantic lives, could not unlock the secrets behind his eyes.

"I understand."

Then he was gone.

## Chapter Three

D'Arcy was seated in the back of a rundown tavern. The wood of his table was splintered dangerously. Beside him, and whispering, was John Mitchel, "Why should I trust you, McGee?"

D'Arcy tried to suppress his anger, but it boiled up and over his face in a flaming red, "I've had enough. You were right. It's time to do something."

Mitchel took a mouthful of whiskey, and studied him for what seemed an eternity to D'Arcy. Finally, "Tomorrow night, right here. Someone will bring you to them."

D'Arcy stood to leave when Mitchel grabbed his arm. The young writer looked at the handful of his coat in the editor's huge, calloused paw, then at the man's clenched face.

"Tell anyone, McGee—your wife, your brother—and you're a dead man. Understand?"

D'Arcy nodded, "I'll be here." He downed the last of his draught, then left.

He never looked back to see his former editor step out of the tavern and onto the street, watching after him. Mitchel grinned with self-satisfaction, then hurried up the street in the other direction.

Deep into the following night D'Arcy, a torn cloth tied around his eyes, was led into a room, and seated roughly into a wooden chair. The cloth was ripped from his eyes.

A single candle was at his side, illuminating only him, and otherwise the room was dark. A half dozen suspicious men hovered over and around him, shrouded by black cloth masks, completely unidentified in the darkness.

It was immediately obvious to D'Arcy that these nervous, lurking men were as afraid of each other as they were of any perceived enemy.

Two men stepped forward. One, obviously the leader, spoke in tones darker than the room, "Do you know who we are, Mr. McGee?"

"I do not."

The leader's voice lowered, "We are the most dangerous men in the history of mankind, because we are not afraid to die for our cause."

D'Arcy nodded, "I understand."

The leader grinned, and the sight raised D'Arcy's flesh.

"No, McGee. You haven't yet begun to understand."

D'Arcy lowered his head, and stared at his hands. They were shaking.

"No one here trusts you, newspaper man. No one likes you either. So you'll understand that before we do anything for you, you'll have to prove your loyalty to us."

D'Arcy, petrified, agreed immediately, "Anything."

The leader crouched in front of the seated D'Arcy. D'Arcy could not have been more frightened of a coiled snake.

"You must burn *The Nation* to the ground."

D'Arcy didn't flinch. He couldn't.

The leader continued, "It's newspapers like yours that offer the Irish an alternative to violent overthrow when there is no bloody alternative!"

"Here. Here," came another dark and dangerous voice.

Standing, the leader paced, "The population will think the British Army did it—they close you every other week anyway. All publications like *The Nation* will be frightened into closing."

D'Arcy glanced around the room at the fearful, silent gathering. When he looked back at the hooded leader, the man was in his face, hissing, "You'll perform this act to prove your dedication to our cause. It will also illustrate to our enemies and our friends that the movement isn't helpless—we can and will respond to force with a violence beyond their imaginings."

Moments later D'Arcy, his blindfold back on, was being led away down the dark street by two men. One disappeared, leaving D'Arcy with the other. D'Arcy felt his mask being removed, revealing the identity of his escort.

He swallowed, "Hello, John."

"Listen to this warning, McGee," whispered Mitchel, "we're told that spies have infiltrated the organization. From this point forward, trust no one."

D'Arcy looked at his former editor. His former friend.

"No one."

Back in the dark room the masked men were still standing motionless, trapped deep in individual thought. Then the leader's voice cracked the silence like a whip.

"Can we trust him?"

There was a pause, then a second, less assured masked man stepped up behind him, "I'd bet my life on it."

"You already have, lad. You already have," said the leader plainly. Then he removed his mask, revealing the most trusted man in D'Arcy's life—*The Nation's* publisher, Gavan Duffy. His face was etched deeply with dark, evil, obsessive commitment. With a twisted take on gentle compassion, Duffy began removing the other man's mask, "But don't go thinking we don't appreciate what you did to get the bastard out here."

Duffy smiled that terrible smile again, right into the barely recognizable, brutalized face of James McGee.

D'Arcy never went home.

He stood in the shadows on the other side of the street from the offices of *The Nation*. He swigged from a bottle of whiskey, working up his courage. He held up a two-by-four with cloth wrapped around the end, and poured the whiskey on it. Then he lit it. The torch exploded into flame.

He stepped out into the empty street, and started slowly across it. Then he took aim at the large ground floor window and let his torch fly. It shattered the glass. D'Arcy turned to run back across. Behind him, the room burst into huge flame. D'Arcy blew across the street from the rush of exploding air, then stumbled into the shadows.

Hidden in the garbage, he glanced back at his handiwork. He felt no pride, only a sickening horror. The sounds of people coming startled D'Arcy to his feet. He was about to run off when he noticed the light from a single candle coming from the second floor of *The Nation's* offices.

"My God! My God, no!"

The roar of Dublin's concerned citizens grew closer, but D'Arcy was frozen till a second explosion rocked the old building.

"God help me." He pulled himself free of his fear and ran across the street and into the blazing offices.

He ran toward the stairs, shielding himself from the flames. The smoke was thick, and he covered his eyes.

"D'Arcy?"

He stopped. That voice.

"Mary?"

She stood at the top of the stairs.

"For God's sake, Mary, what are you doing here! The building's on fire!"

"It's James. He's vanished, D'Arcy. I came looking for him, for you." She stepped forward just as the staircase collapsed beneath her. She fell ten feet.

D'Arcy caught her.

They broke out from the back of the structure and into the dark alley, with Mary still in his arms, coughing. D'Arcy, distraught, mumbled over and over, "What have I done! What in hell have I done!"

Then, as the sounds of a gathering mob started coming from every corner, he put Mary down and yelled at her to run. She stared at him in frightened confusion.

"Please, Mary. Don't let them find you here."

Startled by his behaviour, she began to cry. Then she turned and disappeared into the darkness.

D'Arcy ran back into the building, ripped curtains from the windows, and tried to fight the fire. As people gathered outside, he was sighted by a soldier.

"Who goes there!"

Before D'Arcy could identify himself another voice cried out, "Arsonist!"

The crowd, blinded by their fury, began moving toward the building's entrance, trapping D'Arcy inside. He was forced back into the fire, finally making his way out a huge hole burned through the rear wall.

As D'Arcy ran out into the night one shrouded figure stepped out of the crowd, pointing and shouting "McGee! There! It's D'Arcy McGee!"

The crowd, heeding the call, broke into pursuit. The figure stopped shouting, and pulled the shroud away from his face. His work done, John Mitchel went home.

Bishop Maginn hurried Mary McGee, and James McGee, into his church, and locked the door behind them. James turned to the man in the silk robes, and lowered his head respectfully, "Thanks for setting this up, Bishop Maginn. I know you're not in the habit of harbouring fugitives."

Mary looked up the long, wide aisle, then began to run. D'Arcy stood near the altar, waiting for her. At first they could only hold each other in quiet desperation.

"D'Arcy, they're saying you set the fire."

"I did, Mary. I've made a terrible mistake. I'm so sorry."

James disagreed, "You did the right thing, D'Arcy."

"NO!" D'Arcy shouted, "I have to turn myself in, explain."

The Bishop joined in, "You can't go back now—you're one of them," he offered with cold, factual calm. "I beg you D'Arcy. Leave Ireland before the authorities catch up to you."

"Leave Ireland?" the young writer choked on the words.

The Bishop handed D'Arcy a priest's outfit, "A disguise. A ship called the *Shamrock* is setting sail this very night."

"I will not leave without my wife."

"I can't go with you, D'Arcy."

D'Arcy looked at Mary with disbelief, and she pulled him aside to explain, "I'm pregnant."

Bishop Maginn watched the young couple, whispering prayers one after the other. No man should have to carry the burden of so many decisions in one moment.

"I can't travel on one of those coffin ships—"

"Of course not," D'Arcy interrupted, deep in thought. "You'd lose the baby. Maybe your own life as well. It would be too dangerous. Of course, Mary."

McGee was frozen to the spot. First with terror, and then with a huge grin. "A baby, Mary?"

Her face flickered into a smile, and tears flooded her eyes. Her husband was all the father her child would ever need.

"I'll come to America as soon as the baby is born—" He was kissing her, holding her, pleading, praying, promising, adoring her.

D'Arcy pulled back only inches away from her face, his eyes still on her eyes, when he said, "James. You'll watch over my Mary, won't you?"

But James pulled his brother aside, fidgety with terror and embarrassment, "If they can't find you Darce, they'll come looking for me." D'Arcy stared hard at his brother, then James added, "They'll kill me this time."

Mary stepped between them, her voice steady again, the tears gone, "I have plenty of family in Ireland to look after me, gentlemen—I want the McGee brothers to look after each other."

Bishop Maginn was at the church's main entrance when he jumped suddenly, "The British, D'Arcy! They're here! Go now!" Mary began pushing D'Arcy toward the back of the church. He kissed her once, then desperately stole a dozen more. She was embarrassed, and hopelessly in love.

James opened a rear window, and climbed out through it. He glanced around, seeing nothing and no one, then pulled his brother out after him. D'Arcy reached back for his wife, and whispered, "See that she has your green eyes, Mary."

Mary watched as her husband moved away from the church. She watched as he turned back again and again, waving, smiling bravely, until he vanished into the Dublin night. Just as a dozen British soldiers entered the front door she heard herself whisper,

"God be with you, D'Arcy McGee."

The brothers made their way toward the waterfront, and James could barely contain his excitement, "The New World, Darce—we're going to the land of milk and honey!"

But D'Arcy couldn't hide his true feelings, "I'm running from everything I've ever loved, James. This is the saddest day of my life." The sun was revealing its secrets slowly over the distant horizon, and D'Arcy stopped to look back.

For the last time.

Ireland, as far as his eyes could see.

## Chapter Four

Storms in the North Atlantic had long been the stuff of legend, and it wasn't unusual that a bit of wreckage floating on the waves might be all that was ever known of the fate of a ship, crew and passengers. Two days into D'Arcy's journey the *Shamrock* was rocked by the winds and rains of this unforgiving ocean. Wild and reckless waves slammed into them with such ferocity no one dared move save they lose their perilous grip on some nailed down piece of ship. One hundred and fifty Catholic refugees whispered in private, urgent prayer, certain that their deals with God were all that held the groaning ship together.

With no personal belongings other than their history, the Irish emigrants were also fighting an illness that was holding them captive. With no means of defending themselves against typhus, the ship fever, each morning cast its cold, cruel light on yet more dead.

D'Arcy, disguised as a priest, huddled in a dark corner of the crowded ship. James was tucked into the shadow beside him.

Because D'Arcy was the only 'priest' on board, it wasn't long before the ship's Captain approached him. Against his better judgement, but appreciating the comfort a man of the cloth offered Catholics preparing to meet their Maker, D'Arcy agreed to give last rites to the dying.

Moving from parent to child, D'Arcy quickly learned that the ship's calm and serene pilot was a sympathizer, and revealed his true identity to him. But the politics of Ireland had already disappeared with its coast over the eastern horizon, and the only fear was that the ship would arrive in Boston nothing more than a floating coffin. James had been looking west with positive energy since the boat had slipped off the Irish shore, but D'Arcy kept himself busy so there would be no time to think—no time to remember what he left behind. It was his only solace as another body was dropped over the side, and disappeared forever under the ocean.

Though the fever worsened over the following days, the weather had finally calmed. It was then that a young orphan couple, filthy and impoverished, stepped over to the exhausted D'Arcy holding each other's hands. They asked if he would marry them.

If hope was a flower, the last thing D'Arcy expected to find was this bouquet taking root in the splintered misery of the *Shamrock*. He looked into the lovers' eyes and somehow felt hope for the rest of them. Matrimony was one sacrament D'Arcy could not bring himself to administer in good faith, so he convinced them to baptize their entrance into the New World with the celebration. The captain grinned his approval.

James watched as D'Arcy redoubled his efforts, praying with his countrymen, leading them in gut-wrenching song, and stoking up moral. Finally, with America's skyline breaking the distant horizon, the captain of the *Shamrock* was lowered into the waters off Boston, the journey's final victim.

"Leaving Ireland," D'Arcy told the survivors, "must not be seen as the end of everything." As his tired eyes scraped up along the distant wharf he added, "It must be a new beginning."

James looked at his brother, and smiled.

*America*

# Chapter Five

"This New World has some pretty old buildings," remarked D'Arcy as he and his brother stepped into a rooming house in a run-down part of Boston. As if on cue, wind rattled the old wood. Perhaps it was the last of the North Atlantic wind still caught in the *Shamrock's* sails spending itself wildly through the rooming house, turning the shattered glass and splintered walls into a huge wind-instrument.

D'Arcy and James were introduced to their new 'home' by Maggie Coyle, an old, tough Irish woman. Having dealt with her own kind before, she demanded weekly rents in advance. The McGees didn't have it. Maggie was used to accepting items in trade, but D'Arcy explained that they had nothing of value. It was then she noticed his Irish claddagh wedding band. He hesitated. It had worth to D'Arcy well beyond a weekly rent. Maggie assured him he'd get the ring back the moment he paid up. She was sorry, but... "You can't trust anyone anymore."

Though D'Arcy wasn't at all happy with the arrangement, James pleaded with him to accept the inevitable, "We'll have jobs by morning, Darce."

When Maggie left, gnawing on her silver prize, D'Arcy turned on James, "Mary must never know the ring left my finger for even an instant."

The McGee brothers prepared their battle plan for job-hunting. D'Arcy would go to the finest newspapers, confident there would be work in Boston for a young, ambitious, articulate former editor.

James decided he would take any job offered. He realized his skills were few, but the money he could get for common labour would be his stepping stone to riches! D'Arcy wished his young brother was more realistic, but James' enthusiasm would not be denied. Spirits high, they left their tiny windowless room and stepped out into the Boston workplace.

And a new reality.


D'Arcy found himself in the richly wooded waiting room of Boston's largest newspaper, *The Herald*. He'd waited patiently a long time before the editor finally stepped out, an older, distinguished gentleman—who proceeded to walk right past D'Arcy. D'Arcy's polite grin vanished, and he stepped in front of the man, "Mr. Wilson, D'Arcy McGee." D'Arcy offered his hand, but the editor only glanced at it, and again moved to pass.

But D'Arcy scrambled in front of him, "Mr. Wilson, I've been waiting for you for over an hour. I suspect you can tell I'm just off the boat, but I'm not new to newspapers. I was the editor of *The Nation* back in Dublin, and—"

"We have no need for your kind here," the man interrupted. With that, *The Herald*'s editor walked past D'Arcy and out the door. Stung, D'Arcy stared after him.

"My bloody kind?"

The response to D'Arcy didn't change at *The Boston Globe*. Though he entered with confidence, he exited with a new kind of anger on his face, a frustration that began to cut. He stood a moment in front of the newspaper's huge front doors and pondered how talent alone would not get him a job in journalism in America. He prayed for luck, and stepped back out into the human traffic of bustling Boston.

Twenty minutes and a dozen blocks later, a man standing in front of *The New England Post* wouldn't even let D'Arcy in the door.

James was faring no better. He'd made his way onto a loading dock where men were hard at work moving crates from a docked ship into a warehouse. He approached one worker and asked for the foreman in charge. A huge, pleasant-looking man was pointed out.

James asked the foreman for work, but the man's friendly demeanour changed the instant the young Irishman opened his mouth, releasing his brogue. The man said, "We don't want no trouble here," then turned away.

James followed, confused, "Do I look like trouble? I'm a good worker, hard worker. Strong as a bloody ox." But the foreman had already turned back to his work.

More comfortable than his brother with rejection, James was still motivated when he stepped into a wet, slimy fish-gutting plant soon after. The plant manager met with him, but quickly began shaking his head "No." James gave chase, but slipped and fell on the greasy floor. He found himself face to face with a fish struggling for breath where there would be none. Not having D'Arcy's self-control, James stood and knocked over a huge table, and a hundred pounds of gutted codfish poured onto the floor. Moments later, a huge man threw James out onto the street.

But it was when he approached the foreman of a ditch-digging crew and the burly man pointed to a handwritten note hanging from a piece of equipment that James learned the problem. It read:

JOBS FOR EVERYONE
IRISH NEED NOT APPLY

James read the note, then angrily ripped it off. The workers gave chase, tossing anti-Irish epitaphs as they did. Caught, he was kicked and punched until he fell into a ditch in a cloud of dust. The workers only stared and laughed as James got up, covered in dirt and stink and humiliation, and stumbled away.

A weary D'Arcy walked into a small grocery store, and looked around with confusion. A woman behind a tiny counter asked if she could help him. "I'm sorry, I'm tired...I've made a mistake," he said, "I was looking for the offices of *The Boston Pilot* newspaper." The woman didn't look up from her work, but simply motioned to the back of the shop. D'Arcy looked past a pile of crates to a small door.

In the back room, D'Arcy found a tiny printing press, a small stack of newspapers, and a gnarled, bespeckled old man. This humble operation was all there was to *The Boston Pilot*.

"We've a paid circulation of seven hundred, mostly family," explained the self-defacing publisher named Donahue, "and I do everything here all by myself." Donahue told D'Arcy that if he wanted to work for him, his jobs would be many and varied— from typesetting to inker. But D'Arcy, shaken up by the events of the day, and the nature of this 'back room' publication, stuttered in response. "Not what you expected, lad?" Donahue said with a grin. Then he stood, "Mine's a non-political paper, and I want an editor with your talents to help me build it into something."

"But, you don't know me."

"I'm a newspaper man, Mr. D'Arcy McGee," the publisher said as he tossed a paper at D'Arcy. It was the last edition of

Dublin's *The Nation*, with D'Arcy's screaming headline. D'Arcy sighed, looked at a stack of *Boston Pilot* newspapers, then at Donahue... "Okay, but I'm not going to deliver all of those." Donahue laughed, and D'Arcy smiled.

Then Donahue grabbed a handful of newspapers and handed them to D'Arcy, "No—the editor only delivers half." D'Arcy's grin vanished. "Publisher delivers the other half." Donahue laughed, then turned to leave the small room with his handful of newspapers.

D'Arcy succumbed to his new employer with a shake of his head, then noticed Donahue's hands. They were permanently dyed with newspaper ink. "You'll never get that ink out of your hands, old man."

"The day I do, young D'Arcy—shoot me."

The next morning as D'Arcy got dressed for work, James prepared once more to go job-hunting. Neither brother talked about the overt prejudice they'd faced, but rather, they discussed positively their futures. D'Arcy still wasn't sure about *The Boston Pilot*, but liked the challenge of turning the tiny paper into something. James was happy for his brother. For his own job prospects, James only grinned, "You think maybe I set my sights a little too high?"

The brothers stepped out of their rooming house door, and bumped into Maggie walking past. D'Arcy was happy to tell her that he now had a job, and although the money wouldn't be pouring in, he'd be able to buy back his wedding ring by the end of the week.

"Too late," Maggie said quickly, "I turned it into the local Pawn Shop."

Horrified, D'Arcy demanded the ticket, but Maggie hesitated, stumbled, then admitted... "There is no ticket, Mr. McGee."

D'Arcy demanded to know what happened to the ring, and confused, eccentric Maggie finally told him she'd given it to Stan Shanahan up on the third floor because "We're going to be married!"

The expression of disbelief on D'Arcy's face started James laughing, "I think I'll leave you to deal with this one on your own."

As James set out, Maggie begged D'Arcy not to take the ring back—at least not until the wedding... "Shanahan's a real catch, Mr. McGee. I don't want to lose him."

D'Arcy sighed, "When's the wedding?"

For the first time since D'Arcy arrived in Boston, Maggie smiled.

"Soon as the old bastard asks me."


"We won't be doing business with you even after you're dead!" shouted the coffin-maker just before he slammed his shop's door in James' face.

It was a very tired, frustrated James that walked down the crowded street, hands in pockets. He didn't know where to turn for a job when a seedy-looking character suddenly stepped up, and started walking beside him.

"Looking to buy something?" the stranger asked. James shook his head and kept walking.

"Of course. You look much more the selling type, don't you? Looking to sell something?"

James stopped and looked at the street urchin not much older than himself, "What are you talking about?"

The man pulled him aside and explained in hushed tones, "I'm a fence. Know what that is?" James nodded. "Well, that's what I am. So if you ever want to unload stolen goods, I'm the man to do business with."

James wasn't ready to stoop to crime, and was insulted even to be asked, "What do I look like to you?"

"Irish."

Shocked, James pushed passed the dishevelled man and began walking away.

"They call me Georgie, if ever you'll be asking."

The night fell in huge dark flakes, quickly burying the city. Hidden in this Boston night were D'Arcy and James. They were sharing a bottle of Irish whiskey, sitting on a street curb. As a slow parade of delivery horses made their way past, James was turning all of D'Arcy's questions back on his brother. He didn't need to be reminded of the low points of his day. But he was also proud and hopeful of all the good D'Arcy's editorials might do for the Irish in America.

D'Arcy appreciated the support, "Circumstances the Irish had no power to control have brought us to this sad place in our history. No one will help us lift ourselves out."

"Then we should lead by example." said James, lifting the whiskey to his lips, and the brothers laughed. "Brings me back," sighed James.

"Maybe that's the problem," D'Arcy said as he took another swig. "Brings us all back."

"Truth is, the Irish are hard done by in America," James said. "They live in slums, and are lucky to get work as labourers. Makes you..." he clenched and unclenched his fists, "makes you want to fight for a little respect."

But D'Arcy was thinking less about the good of his people, and more about the good of his family back in Dublin. "Violence was a mistake. The Irish have to stop trying to change the past, James. The future must be a better place to live in. For Mary, and the baby. The world must be made suitable for the innocent."

James stood, and wiped his mouth, "These Americans are not a generous people when it comes to the Irish. They're cheap, and I don't mean with money. They don't offer a shred of compassion or kindness. Not a smidgen of character."

D'Arcy studied his brother, "You've given this some thought."

"It's best we know where we stand, D'Arcy," James sighed. "Come on, I have someone I think you should meet."

Nearly a hundred people crowded a small hall. They listened intently, and cheered wildly, the woman who addressed them. Her name was Maria Monk, and she was on a book tour. The book, *Awful Disclosures of Hotel Dieu Nunnery in Montreal*, was an incredible story. Miss Monk, on tour before similarly packed houses from coast to coast, wearing a nun's habit and carrying a baby boy, claimed to have been raped and forced into the nunnery by an order of Montreal Jesuits!

She was feeding on the anti-Catholic hysteria that the ultra-Protestant mid-1800 America feared more than anything. Monk was sensational, warning the barely restrained crowd of the Catholic's true allegiance to a 'foreign prince'. All in the racist crowd ate it up.

All except the brothers who sat in the back.

James noticed D'Arcy taking notes, and snatched his pencil,."Will you stop being a newsman for one bloody minute and listen to her? This isn't even a political rally—it's a bloody book signing tour!"

"People like this Maria Monk are few and far between," D'Arcy argued. "The silent masses won't condone this."

James grimaced with disbelief, so D'Arcy gestured at the spectacle on stage, "Don't tell me the masses aren't suspicious of someone who puts more effort into selling an argument than making it."

James sighed, "What you don't know about America is a lot. They aren't looking for leaders, they're looking for someone to hate. The Irish aren't welcome here. We have to organize to defend ourselves."

D'Arcy snapped, "Did you learn nothing in Ireland? No man ever won a point with his fists!"

"No, but they won the fight!"

"Then what? Sneaking around in the night like some rat—a wanted man?"

"You could do worse."

D'Arcy looked his younger brother firmly in the eye... "No James, you couldn't do worse."

James smiled slowly. He handed D'Arcy back his pencil, "An editor can't explain what he doesn't understand, but that'll stay our little secret."

D'Arcy couldn't help but grin, "You're an arrogant little bastard."

"And you're all I've got."

As the crowd roared its approval of some inflammatory statement, they grabbed each other affectionately, and walked out.

D'Arcy and James left the Maria Monk speech and poured out into the Boston night with a crowd of angry anti-Catholics. Soon, a scuffle exploded like a brush fire. James moved to join in, but D'Arcy pulled him away. Then three men attacked a passing priest, yelling racist comments as they kicked him to the ground. D'Arcy couldn't believe his eyes, and James had to follow HIM into the fray. The assaulters scurried away. The priest thanked the McGees, and told D'Arcy that these attacks were becoming more common. "They even attacked a NUN in Philadelphia."

James, rubbing a bloodied fist, looked at D'Arcy. He didn't have to say anything.

The following week *The Boston Pilot's* front page headline came off the press with a shout; BIBLIOMANIA!

D'Arcy and Donahue were hard at work when there came a knock at the door. "No produce back here," said D'Arcy without looking up.

"I'd like to subscribe to your newspaper."

The men looked up to see an older Irishman in fine clothing looking back, "It's good to see someone courageous enough to address the situation for the Irish in America. People have been too quiet about the intolerance for too long." The man continued, "Your paper is becoming the voice of the Irish people in America."

D'Arcy and Donahue looked at each other.

"Your name, sir?" Donahue asked.

"McNamee."

"Fine name, McNamee. Isn't that a fine name, D'Arcy?"

"I wouldn't let them call me anything else if MY name were McNamee. Now, where would you like your *Pilot* delivered, Mr. McNamee?" D'Arcy asked the man, grinning hugely.

## Chapter Six

"She's been in labour for sixteen hours," the tired midwife whispered with concern.

Mary was in the bedroom of her mother's home, in the final throes of childbirth. Her face was a mask of sweat and exhaustion, and her mother hovered over her, ever watchful of her precarious condition.

Suddenly, Mary's moan of pain became the healthy scream of a child. As the people in the room scrambled around to see, Mary asked, "Is she all right?"

Her mother laughed, then said, "You tell me, child—she looks just like D'Arcy."

Mary grinned.

Her mother added, "Except she has your eyes."

Mary smiled proudly, and tears streamed out of her big green eyes.

D'Arcy and Donahue were working on *The Pilot's* ancient press when a stack of mail was dropped off. Donahue recognized the writing on one of the envelopes.

"Father O'Rourke, St. Raphael's Parish." The publisher scratches his head, "Influential man, the good Father. Here's hoping he sends his blessings."

D'Arcy could tell from Donahue's tone that this was an important bit of communication. So when the sound of tearing envelope reached his ears, the young editor just went on inking, not realizing his hands were being covered in the blue fluid. He didn't notice the publisher's slow grin.

"Well, then."

D'Arcy looked up.

"It seems here that Father O'Rourke wants *The Boston Pilot's* articulate new editor to come give a little talk to the congregation."

D'Arcy looked almost startled as Donahue stepped out of his own character and into the parish priest's, reading from the letter, "McGee's observations of Irish life in America have not been flattering—he recognizes the prejudice that the Irish are subjected to, but feels they are at least partially responsible. They drink, and there are many arrests due to public drunkenness. McGee's editorials argue that the Irish should take responsibility for their own jobs and futures—take responsibility for the public's perception of them."

Donahue grinned at his writer, but D'Arcy didn't know how to respond. He stumbled through a self-explanation, "I believe that encouraging education and temperance would eventually produce positive results, you know? Get the Irish off the streets and into schools, and public reading rooms—"

"Lad, lad," Donahue interrupted, "You've already sold me. I'm proud of you—always taking the high road, always thinking the best of our people. I think you'd do well to take the good man's pulpit."

But D'Arcy was too self-deprecating to speak publicly, "Thanks, but I'll hide behind my byline."

Then D'Arcy noticed a personal letter in Donahue's pile of mail—from Mary! He ripped it open excitedly. Reading it, his eyes went very big and very round.

Then he shouted.

Publisher Donahue looked over to see D'Arcy as he danced around the room... "What the hell am I looking at?" D'Arcy stopped, and grinned madly.

"You're looking at someone's father."


D'Arcy burst through the door of his boarding house and ran past Maggie. Kneeling in front of her was the very old, very drunk Stan Shanahan. The out-of-breath D'Arcy stopped, spun around, totally oblivious of Maggie's 'precious' moment, and shouted with joy, "I have a baby girl, Maggie! A beautiful, healthy colleen!"

Maggie wanted to respond, but her eyes darted back and forth anxiously between the two men.

"I'm in the middle of something here, Mr. McGee."

"I see, yes. Have you seen my brother?"

"Not for days."

"If you see him before me, don't tell him anything."

"Not a word, I swear."

D'Arcy bounded up the stairs.

Stan Shanahan had fallen asleep on Maggie's lap. A tiny smile of appreciation played across her lips as she gently caressed his grey hair.

Then she hit him on the head.

"I accept," she said brightly into his clenched face.

"That's fine then, that's fine. Accept what, Maggie?"

"Why, your proposal of marriage, Stanley Shanahan."

Shanahan smiled strangely, happy for her, and very concerned and confused for himself.

The moon glowed orange as a hanging lantern as an unidentified man broke into the ground floor window of a three-storey home. Within moments he found a cupboard filled with expensive dinnerware—all gleaming silver, even in the darkness. Into a sack went the heavy collection, and back out the window went the night robber.

Later that same night Georgie the fence was trying to sell some stolen jewellery on a dark side street when he noticed James. The younger McGee was standing on the other side of the street, staring at him. James turned into an alleyway. Georgie interrupted his sales pitch, and walked across the street to follow.
James waited in the shadows with the sack filled with silverware. He produced a solid silver fork to show the fence, and Georgie was very impressed. He told James to give him the bag, he'd take it to some people he knew, and then James would get his share of the 'reward'. James stopped Georgie from taking the bag. The fence played coy, pretended to be insulted, "You don't trust me?"
"I'm Irish, remember? Where I come from, betrayal is as surprising as stewed potatoes."
Georgie shrugged, then with lightning quickness, stabbed James in the shoulder with the silver fork. James collapsed to the ground. Georgie grabbed the bag of goods, and hissed with twisted evil to the fallen James, "Welcome to Boston, you filthy mickey."
Georgie disappeared, leaving James in the dirt, pulling the blood-soaked fork out from his torn shoulder.

D'Arcy was in an Irish bar, very drunk, and sitting all alone. In sharp contrast to his earlier, joyful response to Mary's letter, loneliness had set in.

A shadow engulfed the one he was already in. He looked up, and said softly, "Where the hell have you been, James?"

"Uncle James to you," said James, then smiled.

Then James swooned. D'Arcy saw the blood-soaked shoulder, and stood, "James! What's happened?"

"An accident, Darce. A mistake."

D'Arcy, holding his brother, yelled into the dark, smoky room, "Someone get a doctor, please!" Some in the room shuffled, but none moved.

D'Arcy swung to the bartender, "He needs a doctor!"

The Irish tough stepped out from around the bar with a bottle of whiskey, and knelt beside the McGees, "You'll never get a doctor to come in here, lad." With that, he poured the cheap liquor over the wound.

James bit his lip until it began to bleed.


It wasn't long after that incident that Donahue had D'Arcy on *The Boston Pilot* carpet. He loved his young editor, but was concerned about the new direction D'Arcy's editorials had taken since James' incident. D'Arcy was shifting his comments from Ireland's problems to America's.

"Offending the country you now call home may not be wise personally. To say nothing of the professional risks."

But D'Arcy explained passionately his distaste for the Protestant American emphasis on the bible, "Would they have us believe we were all damned before the invention of the printing press?"

"This Catholic-bashing," the animated D'Arcy continued, "Waving the book of love with one hand and the sword of extermination with the other. A democracy without morality is nothing more than mob rule."

D'Arcy feared that anti-Irish Catholic sentiment would become even more acceptable by the American public if their irrational fears were not dealt with.

Donahue understood, but reminded D'Arcy to "Give it a chance. Things ARE different here. You're in America, not Ireland."

"Not yet," warned D'Arcy.

Donahue took a deep breath, and softened. He knew what D'Arcy's REAL problem was, "How's your brother, D'Arcy?"

"He's disappeared again. Looking for the trouble he knows is looking for him."

Donahue turned away, and mentioned casually, "I heard from St. Raphael's again, and—"

"I've decided to speak to Father O'Rourke's congregation," D'Arcy interrupted. "They mustn't be afraid to strive for something better than is being offered. I understand, it takes a greater sense of commitment to change things than to manage them."

Donahue, obviously pleased with D'Arcy's decision, hid a grin, "It's always been easier to defend the status quo than to promote change. But, a fiery orator like yourself could probably drum up a little faith among them."

"God gave them faith. Men like my brother need hope," D'Arcy said as he returned to work.

He didn't notice that Donahue stared at him with an almost startled admiration for a long, long time.

Georgie the fence was working his corner when a young, dishevelled man stumbled up drunkenly. The drunk tried to get Georgie's attention about stolen goods, but the fence just pushed him off, a little suspicious, "Get out of here, kid, I don't know what you're talking about."

But when the drunk mentioned a stolen box of jewels, Georgie perked up, even grinning through his blackened teeth.

"Where, lad?"

"Just a few blocks away."

The young drunk tripped into the darkness.

Georgie followed.

Moments later, in the shadows behind a shack, the drunk dug up the small box. Once Georgie saw the box, his eyes narrowed. He pulled a small knife from out of his back pocket.

But someone grabbed his hand. Georgie turned.

There stood James McGee, and a small gang of angry looking men. James smiled cruelly. "Thought you might want to meet some of my 'mickey' friends." One brash Irishman threw his bottle at Georgie's feet, where it shattered.

Georgie was trapped. He made an attempt at escape, but was caught immediately.

"Eight of you," he said, fighting for breath.

"No," James smiled, "Just you and me, Georgie."

James didn't just fight the greedy, racist fence.

He taught him a lesson.


St. Raphael's was packed with silent, attentive parishioners. D'Arcy was filled with fire and brimstone. His speech was designed to be inspirational.

"The Irish must fight for what they believe in, not with their fists, but with their minds. We must build schools, build reading rooms, build futures for our people."

Then the Catholic crowd could keep silent no longer—

"Anti-Catholics are everywhere!"

"There is a constant fear of violence!"

"It's easier to do what you're told, and fade into the background!"

"Attracting any attention to yourself only leads to no good."

"Husbands are beat up, the women are threatened!"

D'Arcy raised his hand to silence them. His voice was calm, "The journey to self-realization will be a tough one, but doing nothing is a guarantee that treatment of the Irish will never change." Father O'Rourke, sitting not far from D'Arcy on the altar, nodded in agreement.

Then D'Arcy added, "The people of America will never treat us better than we treat ourselves!"

Suddenly, the back doors to the church were flung open, and a half-dozen stick-carrying thugs stepped in, shouting "Look at all the Catholics, boys—this'll be like shooting fish in a barrel!" The thugs moved forward, and a woman screamed.

But then a second, larger gang of armed men entered, their number crowding the large doorway.

D'Arcy recognized the leader.

"No, James. Not you."

Too late. James and his Catholic gang waded into the half-dozen thugs, and pummelled them senseless in front of the horrified congregation. In no time, someone called out, "Police!" and everyone ran out into the streets.

D'Arcy and James argued late into the night, their voices echoing around the empty, damaged church hall. D'Arcy's efforts to keep his brother from going astray seemed fruitless, "Who are your friends?"

"Men I can trust. Fighting a cause I can believe in."

"I won't argue with you, James, but listen to me. St. Raphael's is going to help me build the Irish Library. A place to go and learn."

James gestured at the damaged church around them,

"Another building where they can find us, D'Arcy? Another symbol of our existence that they can tear down?"

"Don't you see, James? I'm doing what I can to save you."

"Who saved who tonight, big brother?"

James stormed out.

D'Arcy called out after him, but there was no turning his brother back.

The publisher was sympathetic, "You know you were right, D'Arcy."

D'Arcy, distraught, was bearing his soul to Donahue. "I don't want to win the debate and lose my brother. I can't seem to find the words he needs to guide him—I only seem to succeed at further alienating him."

D'Arcy stood, paced, "America is a lot of things to a lot of people—but not the Irish. The hatred already has roots as deep as England. Maybe it's time for me to make my peace with Ireland—go home to my wife and little Martha."

Donahue told D'Arcy he'd already done some preliminary investigating for him. "If you go back now, you may never see your family again. The order for your arrest is still in effect."

Lost, D'Arcy didn't know what to do.

Donahue consoled him, "Your life is in the New World, D'Arcy, not in the old. Maybe it's time for you and Mary to take root here."

Donahue suggested McGee get away for a little while. The Irish community in Montreal, up in the Canadas, had issued a standing invitation to D'Arcy.

"They love your writings, and would like you to come visit as a guest speaker. A more honourable man would probably see this as a healthy break for a friend. But as your publisher, I see this as a wonderful opportunity for my prized writer to sell more *Boston Pilot* subscriptions."

"I've already escaped a British Colony, remember?"

"I've been up there, D'Arcy. Pretty civil people for such an uncivilized climate."

"Then I'll leave them alone. I've got nothing but trouble following me. By the way, any news from the Mayor?"

Donahue shook his head, "You'll get no help with your library from the city. You'll have to build it on your own."

"Then we will," he smiled suddenly. "Because this city doesn't think we can."

# Chapter Seven

Six months later it seemed the whole world had tilted on its axis toward the east coast of America, and Boston Harbour was no exception. Boat loads of immigrants were washing ashore by the thousands during the daylight hours, and more under the cover of night.

D'Arcy stood among the stark-faced newcomers and hills of unclaimed luggage. One boat had arrived from Ireland, and he waited, watched, as dozens of immigrants were greeted by relatives.

Then he saw Mary. She saw him, and froze weakly to the spot. All her packages fell from her arms. She burst out in tears. D'Arcy began to run toward her, tears beginning to stream down his face. As they held each other tightly, he whispered over and over, "Forgive me, Mary. Forgive me."

They held each other a long time in silence. D'Arcy had drifted off in the wash of harbour sounds, the beat of his thankful heart almost drowning them all. Then he realized she was whispering to him, "Nothing was your fault, D'Arcy, nothing. It was all God's will." D'Arcy heard the strange urgency in her voice. He looked into her profoundly sad face, confused.

"Mary...where's the baby? Where's Martha?"

Then D'Arcy noticed that there was no little child standing behind his wife. Mary's lips trembled, and tears started again down her dirty face, but her voice was delicate for her husband's sake, "Martha was very weak, D'Arcy. The trip was...too much."

D'Arcy could not move. The sheer horror of his daughter's death landed on his shoulders like mountains of stone. Then D'Arcy grabbed Mary quickly, and held her in confused, painful desperation, "Oh my God, my baby Martha...a little soul...a little soul I never saw. My God Mary, what have I done to us..."

The couple held onto each other, invisible to an uncaring crowd shouldering their own burdens. D'Arcy and his Mary were together again, and alone, in a strange land.

The rooming house had never looked so bright as the day D'Arcy and Mary watched with smiles on their faces the wedding of Maggie Coyle and Stanley Shanahan. All her roomers witnessed the event with grinning camaraderie. Shanahan was typically abstracted, but as happy as anyone about the festivities.

D'Arcy stepped forward and hugged Maggie, "I'll miss you," he said.

"I'll miss your rent," she said through grinning teeth.

Mary congratulated Maggie. Mary wished her the very best of family life, then couldn't help but catch herself before she started to cry. Maggie pulled her aside...

"Time is everything, Mrs. McGee. For instance—you have plenty of time for more children, but how much longer could I count on looking good enough to catch a man like Stan Shanahan?" She winked, "It's all in the timing."

Mary couldn't help but smile.

Then Mary noticed James as he came in through the back door. He was trying to sneak past the party, but a handful of gold chains fell to the floor. He looked up guiltily, a finger to his lips, signalling Mary to please not say anything. Mary stared at him for a moment, then turned away.

James recovered his stolen goods, and ran upstairs. By the time he joined the gathering his pockets were empty, and Mary was on the dance floor, lost in her husband's arms. She wasn't interested in new, open wounds. Mary was still healing from deep, old ones.

## Chapter Eight

D'Arcy stepped up to an empty, grassy lot just off a Boston side street. He took a good long look at it. Then he nodded his approval.

It was time to build D'Arcy's Reading Room.

The work was back-breaking, and progress was slow. D'Arcy was toiling alone, but it wasn't long before a small crowd of unemployed Irishmen stood off the lot looking on. D'Arcy dropped a load of lumber onto the ground, and glanced up at the gathering. They looked at him suspiciously, and one asked, "What are you doing, you crazy mickey?"

D'Arcy tried to grin, but he was already too sore, "I'm going to build a library. For you. All of you."

None of them moved.

"Can I help?"

It was old man Shanahan. He pushed his way proudly through the young bucks, picked up a two-by-four, and joined D'Arcy. The men watched, but didn't join, as a game but abstracted Shanahan started carrying lumber on his weary shoulders.

"You really think you're going to be able to do this thing, McGee?"

The voice was familiar.

"With you or without you, James," groaned D'Arcy as he dropped a few pieces of timber awfully close to Shanahan's feet.

James turned to the crowd, "I happen to know that he's never built anything before in his life."

D'Arcy straightened, holding his back. Then he reached into his breast pocket and pulled out a couple of sheets of paper. He grinned, "I have a plan."

"Word of advice, carpenter—measure twice, cut once."

D'Arcy appreciated the humour for a moment, then gathered up another load of lumber.

The group of men around James laughed with him. But James turned on them suddenly, flashing a threatening grin, "If you gentlemen aren't doing anything at the moment, perhaps you'd care to lend my brother a hand."

One by one the intimidated men moved out onto the lot, carrying lumber. Shanahan took advantage of this sudden forest of volunteers, slipped out of the bright sun, sat down, and took a deep swig from his ever-ready whiskey bottle.

Mary arrived with a pitcher of cold lemonade, and each worker took a drink. The men were tireless, fully committed to D'Arcy's dream—including publisher Donahue, his sleeves rolled up and sweat dripping into his blinking eyes. He managed a tired grin when he saw her.

"Do you think I can borrow your husband for a few hours, Mrs. McGee? I have a paper to get out."

The publisher and the wife surveyed the lot for a moment, and silently shared the same thought. Even with the sense of purpose, perhaps even destiny, that D'Arcy had instilled among his workers, the project looked like it would take forever. The groundwork was completed, but now the guesswork needed to be more precise. Like D'Arcy, none of the men had ever built a building. Some had never worked at all.

Suddenly, a dozen young men appeared on the street alongside Mary and Donahue. Each carried what looked like a metal weapon.

A spokesman stepped forward.

"D'Arcy McGee?"

D'Arcy looked at them suspiciously.

The spokesman lifted up a copy of *The Boston Pilot*, "This you?"

D'Arcy glanced over at his publisher, and both men looked concerned. Then James moved aggressively by his brother, but D'Arcy pulled him back.

"You've shown you believe in us," the spokesman said in a firm voice. "We'd like to return the favour."

They were carpenters.

Soon, hammers replaced large rocks, and new nails replaced rusted ones. Expertise replaced bad Irish luck.

And hope replaced all other things.


The roof was finally up, and two dozen men were still working hard; hammering, sawing, painting, lifting, shouting.

Shanahan was sneaking a drink from his flask. When the old man noticed D'Arcy approaching, he nervously dropped the glass bottle, and it shattered loudly on the ground.

Everything stopped. D'Arcy looked at Shanahan for a long moment, and the poor old man didn't know what to do.

D'Arcy approached Shanahan till face to face. "I guess the place is christened." Then, he grinned.

Shanahan, relieved, smiled toothlessly.

D'Arcy faced the workers and the curious crowd of onlookers that was now always there, and said, "Shanahan's point is well taken. There will be no drinking on the premises, ever. The Irish will gather here to expand our minds, and our hopes for the future." There was a cheer, then everyone got back to work.

The final touch was the brass doorknob to the front door. Put into place by an especially calloused hand, the worker stepped back to study it. He stepped forward, and spit on it, then polished it right up with his sleeve. Then he turned, and smiled, "That's it. We're open for business."

Fifty people were looking back, and a huge cheer went up. D'Arcy and Mary, Shanahan and Maggie, Donahue and dozens of others fought tears. D'Arcy was sitting on top of the world, and about the happiest Mary had ever seen him.

Off to the side, James noticed his streetwise nemesis Georgie talking to a policeman. The fence was looking through the crowd for James. The younger McGee shouldered his way past the congratulators to his brother, and got right to the point, "Darce, I'm heading out west."

"The hell you are! Just when things are about to turn around for us." D'Arcy said.

James didn't want to be angry, but he was, "I'm not you. But where would we find room on our family mantelpiece for another McGee brother?"

"James, don't pretend you give me no reason for concern."

"Why can't you appreciate me for what I am instead of comparing me to all I am not? All that I can be might not dazzle a man such as yourself, but I might surprise you."

"I hope you live long enough to fulfil your promise."

James, his eyes scanning the gathering nervously, was adamant, "There's a gold rush on, Darce—people are getting rich overnight."

D'Arcy pulled James aside and laid into him, "When are you going to grow up? There's no such thing as leprechauns, no pot of gold at the end of the rainbow. Now listen, Mom made me swear to take care of you James—"

James spit sarcastically, "And you've done a fine job, Darce."

"I've tried to help, James. I built this place for YOU—"

"For me?"

"And what do you think? The Reading Room was built to keep you and your friends out of trouble. If I'm so off with this, you have to tell me something I don't know."

"I can't even read, big brother. That's how much you know."

D'Arcy was stunned silent. James sighed, and then hugged his brother tightly. He whispered into his ear, "I'm dirty, D'Arcy. I don't want to get it on you and Mary."

With that, James turned and walked away. D'Arcy watched in confused silence. Then, "James! What can I do? Anything, just tell me!"

James turned around, but kept walking, "Worry about yourself, Darce—because the next time you see James McGee, he'll be a rich man."

He smiled a forgiving smile, and disappeared into the crowd just as Georgie and the policeman appeared at D'Arcy's side. Still looking around for James, they didn't realize that D'Arcy was staring out after him.

Donahue stepped up excitedly, "D'Arcy, the mayor's here to congratulate you." The spell was broken, and D'Arcy looked at Donahue with weary humour.

"The mayor? There's good politicking for you—come collecting accolades after the sweat's dried up."

But the mayor had a plaque made up without D'Arcy's knowledge, and it was most flattering. The plaque had been engraved, "The Thomas D'Arcy McGee Reading Room." The mayor announced plans to build three more Reading Rooms, and basked in the applause.

That night D'Arcy looked at the hand-carved mahogany with a large smile. Then, his mind's eye drifted back to James.

Only Mary heard him say, "What's the point of saving the world if I can't even protect my own brother."

Their small Boston residence was Mary's home. The new world that D'Arcy had challenged was kept outside by her hand-sewn Tamask curtains, Belleek china, and dainty wool rugs. All had survived the arduous trip from Ireland that Martha had not.

D'Arcy told Mary about James. She admitted that she knew James had been moving with a bad crowd from the first time she'd seen him.

D'Arcy was distraught, "How could I have been so distracted, so pre-occupied?"

Mary suggested that D'Arcy only saw what he was looking for—not always seeing what was actually there.

"Rubbish," he said, and stormed out of the room.

Mary smiled.

A moment later, D'Arcy looked back in, and smiled himself.

His wife was sewing baby clothes.

D'Arcy walked into the Reading Room and found it full of curious and quiet browsers. The only sound came from one especially old man named Butler who was running a gnarled finger along the page of his book, reading the script aloud. Beside him another man sat, listening intently, the poetry of words music to his ears.

D'Arcy walked over to a shelf full of books, and pulled a new edition out of his coat pocket. One of the readers noticed D'Arcy putting it on the shelf, and couldn't help but react.

"*Oliver Twist*, by Charles Dickens."

The reader looked at D'Arcy, and D'Arcy grinned proudly, "Autographed. I saw him on his last speaking tour through Boston."

Others in the room gathered around, very impressed. They stared at the leather-bound volume in its place.

"It's to be read," D'Arcy offered, and a young man in frayed clothing took it out. He took a step away, then turned.

"I can't read," he said.

There was an awkward moment, then the well-dressed McNamee stepped forward, "Here, let me read it to you."

D'Arcy nodded at his favourite subscriber, then noticed Shanahan sitting in a comfortable, overstuffed chair.

"Good for you, Shanahan," he smiled.

The old man grinned toothlessly, and held up his book, "If you see my Maggie, be sure to tell her where I am."

When D'Arcy left, Shanahan opened his book. Inside was a fifth of whiskey, couched neatly in a carved-out indentation. Toasting no one in particular, the old man said, "They'll never respect us if we don't respect ourselves."

He drank deeply, getting more comfortable in his chair.

"Good book, Shanahan?" asked Butler from his own comfortable chair.

"Changed my life," grinned Shanahan. Then he placed the volume over his chest and fell asleep.

# Chapter Nine

*Five Years Later*

D'Arcy sat in a chair with his young son Patrick asleep on his lap. He was far from relaxed however, and glanced nervously at every sound coming from behind the closed bedroom door.

When an infant's wailing started up, D'Arcy tried to stand, and almost toppled the sleeping youngster.

A burly mid-wife stepped out of the bedroom, her sleeves rolled up, and a huge grin on her face, "You have a daughter, Mr. McGee. And Mary is just fine."

D'Arcy didn't say a word. He just sat back down in the chair, a small tentative grin playing across his lips.

Another baby's wail, and Patrick asked from out of a dream, "Who's that, Da?"

D'Arcy whispered, "That's your new sister, Euphrasia." Patrick, returning to fight dragons in his dreams, said, "I love her very much."

D'Arcy smiled, then hugged his son tight.

Little Patrick was squeezing a puppet with huge round eyes with the very same urgency.

The *Pilot* operation had become much more than it was when D'Arcy first joined—a half dozen staffers now hustled about. D'Arcy and Donahue were discussing the next day's headline in front of the still ancient *Pilot* printing press.

"The city's planning on holding an anti-Catholic demonstration," D'Arcy spat with venom, "why would we want to pull our counterpunch?"

Donahue sat down heavily, "All right. Let's hear it."

D'Arcy held his hands up, and sold the headline with bravado, "Philadelphia, The City of Brotherly Love...Catholics Need Not Apply!"

Donahue flinched.

D'Arcy smiled.

Donahue shook his head, but said, "Subscriptions have gone from seven hundred to seven thousand since you got here, D'Arcy. I've got to learn to trust your judgement."

D'Arcy eyed the young typesetter, who went quickly to work. The room was soon noisy enough that Donahue asked what only D'Arcy could hear, "How's your son? How's Patrick?"

D'Arcy was appreciative of the concern, but both men knew the inevitable, "It's only a matter of time." Patrick had always been a frail child, and often fell prey to lingering illnesses. Doctors held little hope he would live out his childhood.

"He loves his little sister so much," D'Arcy continued in a soft voice, "he loses himself with her, she makes him forget how sick he is. They're something to see together."

Donahue realized another change of topic was in order, so he referred to a stack of letters addressed to D'Arcy from Montreal. D'Arcy admitted that the influential Irish St. Patrick's Society was still trying to solicit him for a speaking engagement.

Donahue laughed, "They sure are persistent."

"Mary and the kids might appreciate the holiday," D'Arcy conceded. "She'd never say it, but I've been neglecting the kids, especially Patrick, because of all these outside interests."

Still, D'Arcy was afraid the Irish community in America might feel abandoned by him. His voice was respected, and there weren't many other Irish voices being heard by the general population.

Donahue reminded D'Arcy that "The tour needn't be a lengthy one. Besides, you've already done much to deserve a break." The Irish, with D'Arcy's encouragement, were getting educations. They were attending temperance meetings, and library groups—huge successes with the local communities. "Some might think you're fighting a battle you've already won."

D'Arcy sighed heavily. In spite of his successes, he still felt like a failure—even with his tremendous propaganda machine, *The Boston Pilot*. "The Irish aren't accepted as first class citizens because we don't come from a 'nation' like Germany, France, or England," he said. "We're international gypsies, in search of a land to call our own."

Donahue placed a fatherly hand on D'Arcy's shoulder, "No one man can change the world, D'Arcy. But you've worked hard to change your own small part of it. Take Mary, Patrick, and Euphrasia to Montreal or I'll fire you."

It was winter in Quebec when D'Arcy found himself standing on a stage overlooking a few hundred Irish in Montreal's St. Patrick's Society Hall. He began his speech by telling them about an exchange he heard between a landlord and his tenant back in Boston.

"So the landlord said, 'I'm going to raise your rent, Mrs. O'Finlay.' To which the tenant responded, 'Thank heavens, there was no way I was going to be able to raise it myself'."

The crowd laughed. D'Arcy winked at Mary and young Patrick, who were sitting in the front row.

The joke lead to a serious point, "I see with great pride that the Irish community is flourishing in Montreal. They have money, respect from the community at large, all in all comfortable lives. This is in sharp contrast to the Irish in the United States."

D'Arcy told his rapt audience about the terrible conditions in the States for the Irish immigrants, and what a wonderful example the Canadians would be for them.

"You should set your sights on political office. There are enough Irish in Montreal to elect your own representatives in Ottawa, take control of your own destinies. And if you were to succeed," D'Arcy's voice broke slightly, "this would be the only place in the world where the Irish would have a real home."

After his speech, D'Arcy was approached by some wealthy businessmen, and offered the job! They suggested that if he were to move to Montreal, he could run for public office. D'Arcy was flattered, but said that there was too much work for him to do in America.

Bernard Devlin, Society president, approached D'Arcy with the flair of a politician, "Let's just say that Mr. D'Arcy McGee and myself will stay in touch about the matter."

Then Devlin asked the McGees if they'd like to enjoy some of Montreal's winter finery, "We have a lake on top of Mt. Royal, frozen for skating."

Little Patrick startled everyone.

"Yes!"

Beaver Lake, a man-made pond atop Montreal's Mt. Royal, was enjoying a flurry of skaters. Among them were D'Arcy with Mary and kids—and Bernard Devlin. None of the party except

Devlin were accomplished at the sport, and D'Arcy was ridiculously overdressed—in long coat and top hat.

Son Patrick was carrying his puppet with the bright eyes and huge grin painted on its face. To free his hands for some mischief-making, he tossed the puppet off to the side, and it flew into the lower branches of a leafless tree.

Patrick then threw a snowball, knocking the tall, pompous hat from his father's head. D'Arcy spun. Patrick giggled. Even Mary couldn't help herself. Her snowball struck D'Arcy on the back of his coat, and propelled him uneasily on his skates into a snowbank, where he fell in an explosion of the white flakes. Devlin bellowed. With mock anger clenching D'Arcy's face, he gave his young son chase, and produced an hilarious ballet of imbalance on the ice.

That time, D'Arcy ended up bouncing off of host Devlin, and leaving the print of his rear end in the snow.

As D'Arcy helped the laughing Devlin back onto his skates, Patrick made off with his father's top hat. The hat was huge for his head, and staying balanced on his skates was not as difficult as keeping the thing balanced on his head. Having attracted everyone's attention with his comical efforts, he postured like his father, and repeated a line from D'Arcy's speech, "I've decided to raise your rent!"

The skaters laughed at D'Arcy's expense, and he asked Mary with feigned concern, "Mary, tell me I wear that hat with a little more dignity."

"Maybe just a little more head, D'Arcy." she teased. Then Mary skated away, grinning. He glared at her, and they all burst out laughing.

D'Arcy's expressions aside, his heart swelled at the sight of his son's energy and enthusiasm. Donahue had assured D'Arcy that the most precious thing a parent could give their child was time. Whatever the reason, Patrick, whose days without illness were few, was in joyous remission.

The McGees sat on the snowbank bordering the frozen pond. Mary was holding tiny Euphrasia, and looked on as D'Arcy, on his knees, removed Patrick's skates. The boy's face was frozen, and flushed with a grin, "This has been the greatest day of my life! Da?"

"Yes Patrick?"

"Can we move here? To Montreal?"

"Why? Don't you like it in America?"

"You never have time for Mommy and me in America."

D'Arcy glanced at Mary. She looked away, pretending not to have heard. D'Arcy pulled off a skate, and promised his son, "Something will have to change, Patrick. I promise."

Patrick began to cough violently, and D'Arcy watched with concern. But then Patrick only grinned happily, "I could spend the rest of my life here."

Surprise and sadness registered heavily on D'Arcy's face, but he hid it from his son. Then he picked Patrick up in his arms, "Let's go home."

The McGees passed under the low branches of a maple tree. Perched and forgotten in those branches was Patrick's puppet, wide-eyed and grinning hugely, surveying the scene below. One could almost imagine the puppet was reacting with pleasure to Patrick's voice as it faded away, "I'll always remember this place."

# Chapter Ten

Back in their Boston home, Patrick's condition quickly worsened. One evening he was very weak and pale, but insisted he wash Euphrasia's tiny face before she went to bed. D'Arcy and Mary watched as their four year old son stroked their tiny daughter's soft skin, doing as he'd always done—show heartbreaking concern for Euphrasia. But this time Patrick swooned, and fell slowly to the floor. D'Arcy grabbed his son and carried him into the bedroom.

Moments later when D'Arcy came out, Mary took him in her arms, and they held each other very tightly.

D'Arcy walked with Donahue along the empty Boston street. Donahue casually brought up a disturbing trend he'd noticed, "There are elements of the Irish community that are getting very frustrated about the constant threat of violence against them."

"Nothing new there. That frustration is bred into the Irish like red hair."

"Yes, but they're making noises about striking first."

D'Arcy stopped, and shook his head with frustration. He understood, but didn't sympathize. "It's this penchant the Irish have for drinking to bolster confidence, then going out and committing acts of violence that has so hurt our credibility on the world's stage."

Then D'Arcy heard an old refrain, "They feel that no matter how hard they try, they're never even given the benefit of the doubt."

"They're right, they're not," D'Arcy said. But D'Arcy reminded Donahue that "I supported the violent course once, and now I'm an exile in an almost hostile country. Something some would think I bloody well deserve."

"Sometimes," D'Arcy confided, "I get afraid."

"Of what?"

"For my family. My children's children. The Irish need a place they can call home."

As they turned the corner toward *The Pilot's* office, Donahue stopped, "What's this?"

D'Arcy and Donahue were met at the office doors by a dozen of Boston's finest, including the large and brooding Police Commissioner. He informed Donahue about the burning of Catholic churches in Philadelphia.

"Thirteen people have been killed," he said.

"What's that got to do with us?" D'Arcy asked.

The Commissioner looked right through D'Arcy, then turned back to the publisher, "I believe a pro-Catholic newspaper like *The Boston Pilot* may be in some danger."

"We've never had any trouble before. Are you sure you're not overreacting?" Donahue asked.

Then the Commissioner admitted, "The department has received news of threats made against *The Pilot*."

The news impacted on D'Arcy, "What's happening to this country? A Catholic can't feel safe walking the streets? Don't they remember what became of Ireland!"

One of the police officers passed D'Arcy very close, and as he did, gave him a threatening glare. D'Arcy shut up, and turned to Donahue.

"I'm going home."


They were in a dark corner of the Boston bar, where faces couldn't be identified. These men with their Irish accents were bred of hatred and revenge.

Voices hissed like angry hornets over mugs of cheap whiskey, "The burning of Catholic churches is a hangable offence, and people should be made to pay!"

"When America sees we can give as good as we get, they'll think twice before trying anything like Philadelphia again."

Suddenly, they all fell silent. The man they had been waiting for was entering the room through a back door. He stood over them like a dark lord; a man who exercised unchallengeable power over two worlds.

It was John Mitchel.

D'Arcy's old editor back in Ireland had made the trip across the ocean with one purpose in mind. He was about to make official an organization of Irish fighters that would haunt British Rule around the world for the next hundred years. This terrorist group would come to be called the Irish Republican Army.

But it was baptized on that night in 1857 as the Fenians.

Their first plan was to send Irish-American money back to Ireland in support of the unrelenting, violent overthrow of British control.

"Your identities must remain secret, because your purpose is utterly lawless," Mitchel said. "Your involvement must remain secret even from friends, and loved ones. Remember, for I speak from experience; for every Fenian, there is an informant."

The angry men signed the Fenian pact in their own blood. The first who signed was John Mitchel. He used a knife to cut into his finger, then dipped a writing quill in it. Then he signed his name, blood-red across white parchment. As he did, someone asked, "What do we do first?"

Mitchel's eyes sparked with dangerous fire, "First we must deal with the enemies among us."


D'Arcy stepped through the door of their home, and Mary smiled, "You're home early."

D'Arcy was obviously upset, but Mary had a soothing potion, "We received a letter from James."

D'Arcy looked over as Mary fluttered the letter, "How is he? What's he say?"

Mary handed him the letter, and laughed softly, "He knew I'd ask about a wife. The answer's still no. But he assured me that he has no shortage of women interested in an ambitious prospector—'Women like roses,' he says, 'by the dozen'."

They both laughed. D'Arcy held the letter, unopened, to his chest, grinned hugely, remembering.

Then, softly, to himself, "Could use your confidence now, James."


Shadows skulked around the back of the McGee Reading Room building. These were men with dark clothes and even darker intentions. Suddenly, torches were lit, illuminating the hate-painted faces of the mob. Torches were thrown through the panes of glass, landing in among the books.

Inside the Reading Room, the flames licked along the floor, then up the book stacks. In no time the destructive journey reached D'Arcy's pride, the Charles Dickens volume. Hungry flames engulfed *Oliver Twist*, and quickly turned its pages to ash.

Shanahan was on the big comfortable chair, sleeping off another night of drinking. Smoke curled around him, and flames crawled up from behind the chair.

On Shanahan's wedding finger, D'Arcy's claddagh ring reflected the fiery glow.

A loud banging woke D'Arcy and Mary. D'Arcy walked cautiously to the front door, and opened it. A book lay smoking on the ground. D'Arcy looked around, and saw no one. Then he picked up the book. It was the remains of his Charles Dickens volume. He flipped it over, and carved into the charred and burnt leather cover was the word TRAITOR. He was confused and frightened, but before he could begin to understand what had just happened Mary called from Patrick's room. There was the most agonizing sound in her voice, and D'Arcy came running.

Mary was sitting on the bed cradling Patrick, wiping a trickle of blood from the corner of his rosebud mouth. She looked up at D'Arcy, and her eyes filled with a message louder than words.

Our son is dying.

Feverish Patrick reached for his father, and Mary handed over the tiny, weak body. D'Arcy sang his mother's lullaby, "The Wearing of the Green", and young Patrick asked the same question D'Arcy asked his mother many years before.

"What does the song mean, Da?"

D'Arcy's voice quivered... "It means that there'll always be an Ireland, Paddy."

"Is Ireland a nice place?"

"They say it's the most beautiful on earth."

"Like Canada is for me."

Patrick started shaking, and D'Arcy held him still closer.

"Why do I hurt so much?"

D'Arcy fought to control his emotions, and his utter helplessness.

"I have a way to help you feel better and go to sleep."

"You do?"

"It's magic."

And Patrick's eyes filled with such wonder, D'Arcy had to catch his breath.

"Yes. I have a magic spell that a leprechaun taught me back in Ireland, and if I say it over you, you'll fall asleep."

Patrick's lips quivered into a tiny grin.

"I want to hear it, Da."

"The deal I made with the leprechaun was that no one else could ever hear it—otherwise the magic won't work. I'll have to put my hands over your ears as I say it. That okay, Paddy?"

Patrick closed his eyes, and his father stared into his beautiful face, streaked with sweat. As the tears finally flooded out from D'Arcy's eyes, he put his hands over his little boy's ears, caressing the cheek for a moment. A tiny hand came up and tightly gripped one of his father's fingers. Then D'Arcy leaned over and whispered in a soft, unsteady voice... "I'll love you till the day I die."

Mary, standing at the door behind them, brought her hand to her mouth. Tears streamed down her face as she watched Patrick's grip of his father's finger suddenly come apart.

Then Patrick was gone.


The afternoon sun bleached the California hills like a stinging sand. Slowly, it seemed to suck the life out of everything.

All was silent except for the crackling sound coming from an extremely scrawny, skinned jackrabbit stuck on a makeshift spit, over a small fire.

An old shack had been built nearby into the side of a grassless hill. The grounds around it were littered with the tools of the prospector's trade; charred and rusted pots, pans, shovels, picks, axes, and the such.

Inside the shack someone was scratching around like a scavenging animal.

Out from the shack came a thin, filthy, frightening looking man. His clothes were rags. His exposed face and arms and legs were caked with dirt. His beard and hair were long and stringy. He sat on a rock in front of his rabbit, and poked at it with a stick. Starving, the cooking aroma almost overwhelmed him. Then he reached into his pocket and pulled out a large silver fork—a glittering reminder of a time passed.

This unrecognizable, half-starved gold miner was James McGee.

A strange sound startled him. James jumped to his feet and grabbed a rifle leaning against the shack. He faced a crest in the nearby hill.

"Show yourself!"

A man, looking even worse than James, stepped out. He was staring hungrily at the rabbit.

"This is my claim, private property," James said, his dry voice not very convincing.

The starving man stared at the rabbit, "Claims are worthless—no one I know ever found any gold. But that hare...that hare's something a man can sink his teeth into."

The man started toward the rabbit, but James lifted his rifle, "You've been warned."

Suddenly another, equally dishevelled man appeared behind James, bringing a knife blade to his throat and carefully removing the rifle from his hand.

"Invite us to dinner."

James, his eyes wide with fear, managed to say, "Why don't you stay for dinner?"

In an instant, the two starving men tore into the tiny rabbit like wolves.

James fell to the ground, and watched, weak from hunger.

Days later, James was panning for gold in a tiny stream. He panned with patience, for the millionth time, watching the water sift through the earth—revealing various pebbles and stones.

Suddenly, James noticed something. He reached into the pan, and pulled out a tiny piece of shiny metal. He studied it for a moment. He stuck it in his mouth, then spit the polished pebble back into his hand, and studied it with more intensity.

Shocked.

Confused.

It was gold!

He turned, splashing out of the stream, and ran with all the strength and energy he had left in him. He scrambled up the side of a small hill to a freshly dug hole. He hit the ground on his knees, and began digging frantically with his bare hands. He soon found what he was looking for. Chunks of yellow metal.

James sat down, spit on the chunk of stone, and rubbed it on his ragged shirt. Dirt smeared off, and treasure sparked underneath.

At the very end of his physical and emotional rope, he could only manage a small grin. His white teeth gleamed like gold through his grimy face—and very wet eyes.

A tear streaked through the dirt on his face... "Yes D'Arcy, there are such things as leprechauns. And I've found my pot of gold."

The Boston Cemetery was bleak and sombre. After accepting condolences from a number of mourners, D'Arcy and his wife stood alone over the fresh grave of Patrick McGee. D'Arcy was stoic, while Mary sobbed softly. Suddenly, he began to cry. Mary, almost startled by the sound, held him.

"Patrick's in heaven now, D'Arcy. He's with God."

D'Arcy turned to her, "But now he knows, Mary."

Confused, she wiped the tears from his cheek, "Knows what, D'Arcy? What does Patrick know?"

D'Arcy looked at the grave, his voice softer and sadder than she'd ever heard it, "He knows I failed him. He knows that I failed my family, and my people."

He was falling apart in front of her, and she scrambled to make sense of the pieces.

Although tears once more welled up in her eyes, Mary summoned the spirit that D'Arcy first fell in love with. She grabbed D'Arcy, and forced him to look into her face.

"Patrick now knows what he always suspected, D'Arcy...That his father is not an ordinary man."

His dark eyes finally looked up into hers, and her voice softened, "And he wouldn't have you behaving like one."

They stared into each other, long and hard.

He put a hand on Patrick's tiny tombstone, and whispered as if to his son, himself, or perhaps to the future, "Hope won't come to us. We'll go where hope is."

Then, D'Arcy reached out his other hand to his wife, "Come with me, Mary." As close as she could get to one, considering the pain and sadness, Mary smiled.

"Come with me to Canada."

*Canada*

# CHAPTER ELEVEN

A DOZEN ST. PATRICK SOCIETY MEMBERS, INCLUDING THE PRESIDENT, Bernard Devlin, walked D'Arcy and Mary, and baby Euphrasia down St. Catherine's Street in Montreal. They all stopped in front of a two-storey house. It was a gift from the Montreal Irish community to their promising new political leader. Mary and D'Arcy could hardly believe their eyes. The society wanted the McGees to feel at home in Montreal, and by the look on their faces, they were beginning to feel just that.

Devlin smiled at their responses, and said, "If Mrs. McGee can spare you D'Arcy, I think it's time I gave you a little bit of a history lesson."

The head of Montreal's Irish Society brought D'Arcy back to the St. Patrick Society's Irish Hall. The huge room was empty except for the two men. They walked, and as their heels clicked on the hard floor, Devlin explained the complex politics of Canada in 1857.

"To begin with, we have two Canadas," he smiled. "The Lower is primarily French, the Upper, English. There are three Lower Canada parties; Independent, Rouges, and Bleu, and three Upper Canada parties; Conservatives, Grits, and Reformers. Six people run per riding. The three with the highest vote total go to Ottawa."

D'Arcy listened intently as Devlin continued. "You will run as an Independent, and it should be understood that your biggest competition will be the Irish mentality itself. There are enough Irish in Montreal West to vote you in, but will they trust their destiny to another Irishman?"

"It's my job to convince them they can."

D'Arcy's eyes fell on the flag of Montreal which hung from a banner over the stage, and he caught his breath. The flag was divided into four equal parts, each representing another segment of the city's ethnic population. It had an English rose, the French fleur-de-lis, a Scottish thistle.

And a shamrock.


Montreal was a bustling city in 1857, and especially so on this sunny afternoon. D'Arcy, carrying a wooden crate, made his way through a crowd to a busy corner. He placed the box on the ground, and some passers-by watched the diminutive character step up on it.

An old, bent Irish woman glanced up and shook her head, "Not another bloody Irishman making a speech."

D'Arcy laughed, "It's a new speech."

She looked him up and down, "Maybe it's the soapbox I find so familiar."

Another man called out, "So, what are YOU running for?"

He told them.

D'Arcy's first political speech was smooth as silk, and a tremendous crowd pleaser. The longer he spoke, the deeper the gathering became, "I've dealt with Canada's problem before; the relationship between conqueror and conquered, Protestant and Catholic, empire and nation."

The Irish crowd cheered his understanding, and someone yelled out that they should all vote for "one of their own".

D'Arcy responded, "Don't vote for me because I'm your brother—vote for me because I'm right."

They DID vote for Thomas D'Arcy McGee, and politics in Canada would never be the same.

D'Arcy won!

His supporters gathered in the Irish Hall late, and were crazy with excitement! He tried to quiet the room, but couldn't. He and Mary collapsed with laughter, and the crowd redoubled its cheering. When they finally went quiet, McGee promised his Irish supporters he would fight for a New Nation that would guarantee the rights of all people—including the sad nationless gypsies of the 1857 world, the Irish. Cheers were once more deafening.

McGee reached for Devlin in the crowd, and the two men hugged. The people loved it. Then there was a brief exchange between the two men that caught Devlin by surprise.

"I've just heard that a substantial amount of Montreal Irish have been supporting the violent overthrow of British rule in Ireland by sending cash back to the old country," D'Arcy whispered urgently.

Devlin was suddenly awkward, confused, "Is the new Member from Montreal West asking because he supports it?"

"I was hoping you'd help me put a stop to it."

Then D'Arcy was pulled away among his admirers, leaving Devlin to stare after him. When another senior supporter passed, Devlin grabbed him and whispered, "We may have a little less than we bargained for with McGee."

D'Arcy and his wife stood and surveyed the Montreal night from their rooftop, having escaped the party below to spend a moment together. They were both filled with renewed hope for their future. There was just enough music seeping out into the night for them to dance to. They waltzed across the rooftop, two silhouettes against the moon.

The sound of shattering glass stopped them. D'Arcy peered over the roof's edge overlooking bustling St. Catherine's Street to see a few hoodlums smashing his windows with bats and rocks. Then they ran off, chased by McGee supporters. Mary was concerned, but D'Arcy was still grinning, "Devlin said to expect something like this. Nothing's unanimous in this town."

"That's not altogether true," she said with a romantic smile. Then, with what seemed to be the entire city playing music just for them, the McGees returned to their dance.


The Parliament Buildings in Ottawa would someday be one of the most intimidating structures D'Arcy would ever see. To his eyes, more accustomed to the flat green fields of Ireland, the broad-shouldered monolith bullying its way up into the skyline would have a peak tall enough to puncture the heavens and stir the stars.

But that building would only exist in a half-dozen years. This was 1857, and the seat of government was less grandiose and romantic than it would someday be. Still, it froze him to see it.

When he took his seat inside, D'Arcy was again overwhelmed. This time by the utter silence of the regal House in Ottawa. Lost in his own world, D'Arcy didn't even hear his name when it was recognized by the Speaker.

He heard it the second time, "Member from Montreal West, Thomas D'Arcy McGee!"

Startled, D'Arcy stood. He looked around, attempting to take in the room's grandeur, attempting to gauge the temperament of the august politicians who filled it. He took a deep breath, and began.

D'Arcy needn't have worried—it was an outstanding speech. His poetic grasp of language, and painfully simple grasp of common sense, held the room spellbound. With fearless, brutal honesty, he urged bolder policies upon the government, "A new nation, less obsessed with the distinctiveness of its parts, more concerned with the fair, respectful integration into a single community—a Canadian community."

Incredibly, John A. MacDonald left his seat as leader of the government, and walked across the floor toward him. D'Arcy didn't know if he was expected to stand, or run. Then the Prime Minister reached out to shake D'Arcy's hand.

The huge gesture sent murmurs through the House, and would bind the two men through thick and thin, forever.

In the luxurious offices of Prime Minister John A. MacDonald, the two men introduced themselves. After exchanging a few pleasantries, MacDonald explained to the cocky young Irishman that, "You've made a powerful enemy out of George Etienne Cartier."

Cartier was a Quebecer D'Arcy defeated for his new seat, and the francophone would later be remembered with MacDonald as the co-architect of Confederation.

D'Arcy joked, "If I had a penny for every enemy I've made in this life, I could afford to quit politics."

Charmed, MacDonald was compelled to ask D'Arcy about his association with the violence in Ireland.

D'Arcy glanced at the Prime Minister. "Does the Prime Minister believe that if he were to scratch ANY Irishman, he'd find a thug underneath?"

MacDonald smiled, "I'm sorry. You're right. Please understand, some of my best friends are—"
"Irish?"
Taken aback, MacDonald looked at D'Arcy. The fiery-eyed Irishman grinned. MacDonald shook his head, "Got me, again. Pre-conceived notions. I'm sorry."

D'Arcy then explained that he wasn't ashamed of his earlier 'career', describing the individuals in the political movement as a "Pack of fools, but honest fools." Then, more whimsically, "It was a coming of age, a loss of innocence."

"I believe that loss will become this country's gain," flattered MacDonald, "and we look forward to your opinions in the House." He stood from behind his large mahogany desk, and walked passed the huge velvet-draped windows, "I understand you're studying Law at McGill," asked MacDonald.

"I wanted to help maintain what I believe to be a wonderful tradition in this northern land—all members of Parliament must have university degrees." It was less presumptuous on his part than practical, however, "No harm in having a career to fall back on if politics doesn't suit me."

MacDonald smiled, "Politics suit you just fine." The Prime Minister moved to a tray with crystal decanters, "Can I offer you a drink, Mr. McGee?"

"I can't," he said. Then, "I promised my wife."

MacDonald looked at McGee with warmth, "I understand."

"Except of course on special occasions," said D'Arcy with a straight face.

With that, D'Arcy turned toward the door, leaving MacDonald looking after him in confusion. Then D'Arcy stopped, as if remembering something, "Oh, they also say the Irish have a quick, dry wit." D'Arcy flashed a grin before he vanished.

MacDonald let out a huge laugh, and shook his head, "If nothing else, he'll keep us on our toes."

On March 17 of 1857, a huge St. Patrick's Day parade travelled down its City of Toronto route. This was an Orangemen's Parade for Toronto's Protestant majority. It was also an indication of the country's religious struggle.

A fight broke out with some Catholics, and a man was stabbed with a pitchfork, killing him instantly.

This terrible news made every paper from coast to coast.

D'Arcy was on an Ottawa night train, bound for Montreal. He was holding the *Montreal Gazette* in his hand, and reading the headline about the Toronto incident. He'd wrung the paper into ribbons before the train had reached its destination.

D'Arcy got off the train, and was startled to find himself met by a large group of enthusiastic supporters—ten thousand people—led by Bernard Devlin himself. News had reached them that their Irish representative had done them proud in Ottawa.

But one reporter took advantage of the very public moment to address the parade murder in Toronto. "Is not the growing Fenian cause correct? Shouldn't the Irish Catholics take up arms to protect themselves?"

"Absolutely not!" D'Arcy said definitively.

Devlin was trying to reach D'Arcy to quiet him, but the wily reporter baited the young politician once more, "Need I remind you sir of the pro-violence stand that got you exiled from Ireland? Are you now turning your back on Irish suffering?"

Denying that his dramatic shift in opinion now made him a traitor to Ireland, McGee explained, "Good judgement comes from experience, and experience comes from bad judgement. I was a very young man, and my vision was blinded by hatred. But no Irishman has the right to bring his problems to this foreign soil. To move ahead with optimism and enthusiasm Ireland must forget her past, and I must be permitted to forget mine."

As Devlin tried to hide his shock and surprise, D'Arcy continued, "And don't be fooled by those who would have you believe that anti-Fenian means anti-Irish. I am pro-Irish, and anti-violence. We must understand how, in these troubled times, the difference may be a subtle one to cultures other than our own. But the vast number of Irish are peace-loving people who deplore being bunched together with a small group of misguided hoodlums."

There were cheers, but some in the crowd were confused, and the damage had been done. Devlin smiled bravely, and lead D'Arcy away. In a hushed whisper, Devlin explained, "D'Arcy my boy, here's your first lesson in politics—Dance with the one who brung ya."

"Meaning?"

"These good Irish people voted you in. Your job is to tell them what they want to hear."

D'Arcy stopped walking, and looked at Devlin, "I'll not be a puppet to any interests other than the ones you invited me here for, Mr. Devlin. As far as I'm concerned, what's good for the Irish people is not a matter for debate."

Devlin watched D'Arcy walk on, and he wasn't pleased. But of far greater consequence to D'Arcy McGee, the Fenians would never forgive him.

D'Arcy entered his home a short time later, and Mary greeted him with a smile, "I have a surprise for you, D'Arcy."

"I could use a happy surprise, for a change."

Mary looked toward the parlour, and D'Arcy's confused eyes followed.

There stood James.

But not a James that D'Arcy had ever seen before. This one was a dandy, wearing the most expensive and showy suit of the day—and a big, crowd-pleasing grin.

James regaled D'Arcy and Mary with his exploits. It was an animated, hilarious, self-defacing monologue. James had struck a huge gold mine, and turned his profits into a West Coast shipping company. He was in the pink, and his future looked just as rosy. He admitted that his letter had been a lie, full of hope and wishful thinking. But now he was living proof that his quest was true.

D'Arcy could not have been happier for his brother, "But you know how much I like being proven wrong."

James readily admitted, "You were right, big brother. My good fortune is the exception that proved you right. I beat a one-in-a-million shot."

James had brought gifts for everyone, including Patrick. As D'Arcy looked awkwardly at the puppet—exactly like the one the youngster used to cherish and had lost in Montreal—Mary decided she'd leave them alone for a moment, "I'll make us something to eat."

D'Arcy held the puppet close, "Patrick's dead, James. He's buried in Boston."

James was thunderstruck, "I'm sorry, I didn't know. Only a few letters caught up with me. I should've been easier to reach."

D'Arcy handled the puppet with its wide eyes and irrepressible grin, "Me, too."

Mary entered the room slowly, and James looked at her, then cleared his throat, "I'm sorry Mary. D'Arcy."

"I'm the one who's sorry, James."

Mary stepped in before D'Arcy got lost inside of himself, and invited the men to the dinner table.

It was a simple table, but covered in food. James picked up the humble table ware, "Next time I come by Mary, it'll be with a set of silverware that'll blind you."

Mary's expression made him wink. "And I won't be plucking it off someone else's table, either," he added.

They laughed.

James suggested that maybe D'Arcy should consider coming out West, to seek his fortune, "Now that I've taken the risk out of it—I could use a good man like you."

D'Arcy looked at Mary, who hid her grin. Then D'Arcy turned back to his brother, a mixture of pride and irony, "Oh, how the tables have turned."

D'Arcy pushed himself away from the table, "I have work to do here. The Irish need a country, and—"

"The Irish already have a bloody pope, D'Arcy! Get off your high bloody horse and start living your life for yourself." He leaned across the table, "Tell me—how much money does this politician's job pay you?"

Again, D'Arcy looked at Mary, then back at James, "Nothing."

James was genuinely shocked, "Nothing, Darce?"

"That's right. Only Ministers get paid. And only members of the ruling party can become Ministers. I'm neither."

James stood, shook his head, anger mounting, "No, I was wrong about the Pope. You're bloody Moses himself, leading his forgotten people through hell with only the shirt on his back."

"Sit down, James. Behave yourself."

James did, still staring at D'Arcy in disbelief. Then, "Well, I think you should know I've decided to throw my support behind your political opponent."

"That should cost him the election," D'Arcy quipped, and the brothers laughed.

Then James looked at Mary, "Mary McGee, how do you explain your errant husband to the neighbours?"

Mary walked past James and put her arms around her seated husband, "My husband's building a country." They looked lovingly at each other, and fell into a romantic kiss.

James looked on, feigning disgust, "Well, it must be love then. Working for free. Anything less than love and she'd be serving your head on this platter, an apple stuck in your mouth."

Then James' voice took on a serious tone, "Does he have what it takes to build a country, Mrs. McGee?"

"I think Thomas D'Arcy McGee can do anything," she said, looking at her husband's face.

"I'll tell you this, if my brother could capture the imagination of a woman like you, he probably CAN do anything."

It would be years before D'Arcy heard from his brother again.

## CHAPTER TWELVE

### 1861

D'ARCY PASSED A PAPERBOY ON AN OTTAWA STREET, WHO WAS crowing, "America goes to war with herself! American Civil War! Read all about it!"

D'Arcy paid for a copy of the *Ottawa Citizen*, and read the headline, "Union Soldiers Move Against South."

D'Arcy worried aloud, "James."

James and an associate were sitting in the open side of a cargo car parked among others in a train yard. "The Confederate Army has cut off all free trade between the North and South," said the older, bespeckled man.

"What about my trains?"

"They were all blown up, James."

James jumped down from the car, and paced around, thinking, "You know, the debt I'm carrying—"

"I know, James."

"—They'll throw me in jail for the rest of my life."

The associate lowered himself stiffly off the train, "If you're looking for a place to lay low for a while, I know just where."

"I'm listening."

"The Union Army."

At first James looked like he'd burst out laughing. But then his expression changed. He began clenching, and unclenching, his fists.


MacDonald was holding a strategy meeting with a large representation of Upper and Lower Canada government officials in an Ottawa boardroom. The topic was a unified Canada, and how to sell it from coast to coast. The Prime Minister discussed the benefits to the nation such a country would enjoy, "A national railway, population growth, development of natural resources, uncovering new mines and minerals, and securing trade to the West. Can any of you suggest other selling points?"

D'Arcy added the importance of naval and military strength, "The United States, in the middle of a Civil War, can no longer be considered a peaceable, non-aggressive country."

MacDonald smiled. Once more he liked the arguments he was hearing from the young Irishman, "Perhaps I could prevail upon you the task of building up support for a Union where it is now enjoying it the least—New Brunswick."

It wouldn't be the last time the Prime Minister of Canada reduced a roomful of important politicians to hushed whispers over his confidence in D'Arcy McGee, a man not even in his own, ruling party. The Independent from Montreal West agreed to go ahead of MacDonald, and test the cold eastern waters.


Leaving the Commons Chamber D'Arcy met a merchant friend, back from a business trip in the U.S, "Any word of James?"

The merchant produced a document, and handed it to D'Arcy, "James McGee's company went broke, and he was last seen two months ago. Your brother's wanted by a number of banks and investment firms for defaulting on his loans."

D'Arcy sighed heavily... "Where would he go?"

Buried deep in the thick forests and abandoned farm fields of the northeastern U.S. were hundreds of boot camps. Civilized and uncivilized men struggled through various drills. Guns were being fired, and men charged with bayonets. Officers moved about, barking orders and building character. They were shaping Union soldiers.

Among these men was James McGee.

He was marching in formation with soldiers dressed in their uniforms. Marching beside James was Calvin Book, a violent, dangerous man. He whispered to James as they marched in file... "Know how I get myself worked up for killing Confederates?"

"Tell me."

"I pretend they're Irish." Then Book smiled a vicious, toothless smile.

In was a windy fall evening when D'Arcy stood at the podium in front of a large hall. The room was full of representatives of the Irish community in New Brunswick. His topic, which was agreed upon ahead of time in the hope it would most entice these Maritimers, was the "Intercolonial Railway in Relation to the Future of British North America". There were stirrings of sympathy for D'Arcy's dream for a Confederation that raised his hopes.

But he was also challenged.

In the room was the editor of the province's premiere Irish Catholic newspaper, *The Freeman*. His name was Timothy

Warren Anglin. Little did either man realize at the time that Anglin's initial fight against Confederation would eventually cause him to challenge D'Arcy for the leadership of the nation's Irish.

The room was crowded with passionate argument. Leaders of the community argued the local benefits of Confederation. Editor Anglin was concerned that the Maritimes would be poor second cousins if immersed in the much larger scheme of Confederation.

Anglin was pushing for a local railway, while D'Arcy argued for the Intercolonial Railway.

"With all respect due his suggestion," D'Arcy said, "Mr. Anglin's opposition appears selfish and short-sighted."

D'Arcy had taken the bait, and Anglin tugged hard on the line, "May I suggest that D'Arcy McGee is a visionary ideologue who should come down from the clouds long enough to deal with concrete reality."

It was a wonderful debate.

D'Arcy was typically articulate in defining his dream of a new nation, and the emergence of a CANADIAN identity, "A Canadian nationality, not French Canadian, nor British Canadian, nor Irish Canadian. That is what we ought to labour for, that is what we ought to be prepared to defend to the death."

Anglin scoffed, "And what will account for the internal differences in your new nation?"

"Tolerance," said McGee.

Anglin dismissed the concept out of hand.

McGee exploded, "I condemn the introduction of Irish questions into Canadian politics!" Then he spun to confront his fellow Irishman, "We grew up in Irish towns where Catholics and Protestants took separate coaches to Dublin," D'Arcy said, allowing the memory to sting the crowd. "Did you know that in 1790 the Catholics of Montreal accepted newly arrived Presbyterians by giving them one of their own churches to worship in?" He again challenged Anglin directly, "Find me a better example of true tolerance in the history of any other country—and I'll move there!"

"Here! Here!" came a voice from somewhere inside the gathering, and D'Arcy smiled. And then his voice softened, mellowed, and he held out his arms as if to embrace them all.

"With dreams such as ours, a united Canada from coast to coast, we must allow ourselves to have faith in things as yet unseen. So, let's not quote politicians when we can paraphrase the poets." D'Arcy voice rose, "Let us aim for the moon. Then, even if our grand scheme fails, our new country will still fall among the stars."

Anglin, for the moment, had been silenced.

McGee, the man who would later be eulogized as the "Most eloquent voice of the Fathers of Confederation," strode off the stage, leaving the crowd in his wake.

D'Arcy met John A. MacDonald at the Fredericton train station, "Welcome to New Brunswick."

MacDonald had been reading Editor Anglin's attacks against the Confederation idea in his newspaper, *The Freeman*, and suggested that maybe some of the attacks against D'Arcy were getting personal.

D'Arcy laughed, "Put one Irishman on the spit, and you'll always find another to turn it."

The very next night while MacDonald was addressing a gathering of local government officials in the Fredericton City Hall about the benefits of Confederation, news reached them of an attack. A group of heavily-armed Fenians had landed in New Brunswick in the early morning hours. But the numbers were so small, they were immediately turned back. The meeting broke up to investigate the matter.

MacDonald looked at D'Arcy who shrugged with confusion—he had no explanation for the sudden, radical behaviour of some American Irish.

D'Arcy and MacDonald left the building, and were immediately and very publicly confronted by Anglin. *The Freeman* editor loudly accused McGee of orchestrating the pathetically under-equipped attack to drum up support for Confederation, "If New Brunswickers feel sufficiently vulnerable to hostile attack, they'll want the larger Canadian military defending them!"

D'Arcy was outraged, "I deny the charge! I know nothing on any personal level of the people associated with the failed military attempt on New Brunswick. Why would I? The charge is preposterous!"

Anglin claimed to have in his possession a list of believed Fenian sympathizers.

D'Arcy, disinterested, walked past, but Anglin whispered close enough that only D'Arcy and MacDonald could hear, "Does the name James McGee mean anything to you?"

Outraged, D'Arcy lunged to attack the editor, but MacDonald and others pulled them apart.

MacDonald pulled D'Arcy back inside the City Hall to argue more privately.

D'Arcy sputtered, "I'll sue Anglin for slander!"

"You will not," MacDonald counselled, "the whole incident should die down as soon as possible." Then, pacing, "This incident never happened. Understand?"

D'Arcy looked at MacDonald with disbelief, "My brother had nothing to do with this!"

"We know."

D'Arcy's expression changed, "Know what?"

MacDonald was embarrassed to admit, "Your brother's fighting with the Union Army out of Boston."

D'Arcy was shocked, "James is fighting?" He was silent for a moment, then, "You've been checking up on me, Mr. Prime Minister. I'd hoped our insecurities were behind us now. I've told you the truth—"

MacDonald interrupted angrily, "D'Arcy, what's the truth got to do with anything! Politics is all public relations. It's the public's perception here that will hurt us."

Outside, Anglin was grinning when D'Arcy passed him. D'Arcy glanced back at the editor, and Anglin shrugged, "I'm just trying to think of something nice to say to you."

"Good night would be music to my ears."

D'Arcy had made a lofty opponent whose crafty manipulation of the situation at hand would bring national attention to Anglin and his causes.

D'Arcy arrived home from Ottawa, flushed with scars from his recent battles. He and Mary had not seen each other in many days. She listened and learned about James, and Anglin, and decided to work D'Arcy's anxieties out of him.

She flirted D'Arcy into distraction, "Perhaps the Member from Montreal West is too tired?"

He was defenceless, and teased in turn, "The prowess of Irish men is a well known fact."

Her eyes twinkled, "I've heard rumours." She turned into the bedroom, his eyes stalking her. He began untying the knot of his dress-black scarf, and turned to follow.

Hundreds of miles away in a Pennsylvania brothel a flamboyant madame addressed six Union Soldiers, laying down the rules of behaviour. When she told the men and her girls to pair off, one young hooker pointed at one particularly handsome soldier.

"I want him," she said.

The soldiers parted, revealing James McGee sitting behind them, drinking.

As D'Arcy and Mary made love, James and the young hooker had sex. D'Arcy and Mary's lovemaking showed compassion, gentleness, and respect.

"Mary," he whispered, over and over.

James was almost brutal with the hooker, as if she expected the treatment. The first word he spoke was a grunt, "Name?"

She replied, "Got one you like the sound of?"

D'Arcy and Mary's passions were escalating, and both were close to losing control. Mary was now repeating her husband's name over and over, D'Arcy D'Arcy D'Arcy 'Daddy'.

Daddy?

Mary and D'Arcy sat upright. Young Euphrasia was at the bedroom door. When she saw her father, her face lit up, "Daddy!"

Euphrasia jumped into her father's arms. D'Arcy and Mary exchanged helpless glances, and she said, "Everyone wants a piece of D'Arcy McGee."

D'Arcy succumbed to the little heart... "I love you child."

In the same dark, but of a Pennsylvania night, James uttered more than a single grunt in passion. The young hooker responded with shock to the brogue in his voice.

"You Irish?!"

James was confused, "What?"

The hooker drew the covers over her, and her face clenched with hate, "Are you goddamn Irish?!"

James was standing now, facing the irate girl. He snapped, "Are you kidding me? A bloody whore?"

The girl grabbed a pottery bowl by her bed and threw it at him. It smashed into pieces against the door behind his head.

"I may be a whore, but that doesn't mean I have to sleep with a filthy Irishman!" She pulled a gun out from under the bed; a large gun in her small hands, and pointed it at him.

James lifted his hands and backed away, "Killed by a harlot? If my dead mother ever found out, she'd murder me."

"Too good for a goddamn Irishman," she hissed.

James put some money on her dresser, and grinned, "You're the best money can buy."

He was gone.

At D'Arcy's next visit to the House of Commons he hit back at his critics with scalding bolts of verbal lightning. His own history had made him the government's front man in the battle against such things as the Fenian raid on New Brunswick. He was utterly ruthless in his condemnation of the violent society.

D'Arcy argued that the Fenians were society's best argument against the Irish as a civilized people. "How easy it is for one grand and terrible act like that perpetuated against the good people of New Brunswick to turn opinion against the many and good efforts of North American Irish society," he announced with passion.

The Fenian mentality was destructive, explained D'Arcy, "They'd have you believe there is a member of the secret society sitting across the dinner table in every Irish home—prepared to eat their own young like wild animals if need be. This is a gross exaggeration."

Then his voice assumed a different, deeper tone, "But if it were true, and even if my own brother were a Fenian, I'd turn him in for the good of my country."

The ovation was tremendous in the House that day. But the repercussions were to be even more deafening.

Late one night in MacDonald's office, the Prime Minister invited D'Arcy to run on the Conservative ticket. He wanted the eloquent Irishman onside as they prepared the final offensive on the Confederation debate.

D'Arcy accepted. Now all he had to do was convince his electorate back home in Montreal West that the move wasn't personal opportunism, but the appropriate political strategy. MacDonald knew that D'Arcy had ostracized much of his Irish support with his blatant condemnation of the Fenians. Many felt his comments had not worked toward bringing the community together, but rather, had proved divisive.

And D'Arcy knew the source of this perspective, "Anglin's selling the notion that I want to save the Irish from themselves—for the good of the British Empire."

They also knew that this had rallied many of D'Arcy's old friends around editor Anglin. The New Brunswicker had even decided to run in the federal election, "If there ever is one."

"Could make for some interesting moments in the House," D'Arcy offered.

"Politics sometimes create strange bedfellows," MacDonald said. Then he added, "Look around for new friends."

D'Arcy took a deep breath, then grinned at the Prime Minister, "This close."

D'Arcy held up his thumb and forefinger, and MacDonald asked, "That close to what?"

"This close to having that drink you offered me back in 1857."

# Chapter Thirteen

Gettysburg had been the sight of an horrific battle, and many soldiers had been accidentally left behind in the carnage to die. Among them was James, crumpled at the foot of a tree, blood streaming from a shoulder wound. Shock had set in, and he couldn't move. His Union Soldier uniform was caked with mud.

Suddenly, someone was standing over him. James turned with much painful effort to see a Confederate Soldier aiming his rifle at him. James was in so much pain, he could just mutter, "Do it."

But the Confederate recognized the brogue, and lowered his weapon. He, too, was Irish.

In the confusion and frustration of this American Civil War, the Irish had become separated by an ideology that meant nothing to them. The Rebel soldier handed the unarmed James his pistol, and turned to walk away.

A shot rang out, and the Rebel soldier fell face down into the swamp. James' Union nemesis, Calvin Book, appeared out from behind the thick trees. "Looks like my luck's changing," he said cruelly, "getting a Confederate and an Irishman with one shot." James felt the rootless, flightless danger of the soldier set free, and knew he was going to be killed next.

But the Yankee was disturbed by the sound of the Rebel struggling to get up. Book turned, and moved toward him, "Too stupid to know when you're dead?" He lifted his gun for the 'coup-des-grace'.

A bullet hit him in the back, and Book was dead before he hit the ground. The thankful, frightened Rebel looked passed the fallen Yankee.

James, using the Rebel's pistol, had shot Book. Both wounded soldiers stared at each other in silence. Neither could move, neither could escape the evidence of the murdered Union Soldier.

James muttered, almost to himself, "They'll want to know what happened."

The Rebel, also moaning from pain, said, "Don't worry—we'll both be dead before that problem gets here."

Then, the Rebel introduced himself, "Kieron Donovan."

"James McGee."

"See you in hell, Irish."


The New Brunswick offices of Anglin's *Freeman* newspaper were far less humble than the *Pilot* operation D'Arcy had worked in Boston. Anglin was using this resource to the fullest, responding to McGee's new Conservative candidacy in its very public forum. He grinned like the cat who caught the canary as he wrote...

"*Habitual lying is deeply disturbing in a grown man, even a politician, where reputation is the coin of the realm. Truth is not a device to be trotted out when it suits your needs, to be hidden when it doesn't.*"

In Montreal, Society President Bernard Devlin, in anxious, concerned contrast to Anglin, read the rest of Anglin's editorial with growing anxiety, "There are twists and turns in Mr. McGee's past, and his technique has been to suppress, to deny, to fabricate. Mr. McGee is exactly as good as his word. And therein is the problem."

Devlin threw the paper down, and sighed deeply. A moment's reflection changed his expression, and he turned to one of his staffers and said, "I think it's time we made Mr. Anglin's acquaintance."

McGee, his unruly hair curling like black smoke around his head, stood in the Irish Hall before a hostile crowd. Running once more for his Montreal West seat, D'Arcy was quickly challenged by someone in the crowd, accusing him of being a political opportunist.

"Which way's the wind blowing today, McGee?"

D'Arcy responded, "My position on Fenianism could not be clearer. I have no intention of stirring up foreign political animosities on Canadian soil, and the silence of the Irish community concerning these hoodlums condones it. I don't see the virtue in the Irish trading away their future for their past— Sleeping with the devil you know rather than the angel you don't."

Heckles continued, "Mr. Anglin doesn't find it necessary to turn on his own people to win votes!"

And, "Timothy Anglin isn't kowtowing for the Scottish and British vote!"

And, "How do you respond to Mr. Anglin's charges that you no longer speak for the Irish community—but against it?"

D'Arcy moved to answer, but his head began spinning at the chorus suddenly erupting around him...

"Anglin! Anglin! ANGLIN!"

It was in the same hall, with the same audience, only two weeks later, that the call rose again...

"Anglin! Anglin! Anglin!"

But it wasn't D'Arcy standing at the podium, it was his Irish rival from New Brunswick, Timothy Anglin. The man was smiling broadly. He was making an impassioned speech that contained an obvious reference to D'Arcy's new political style, "I don't find it necessary to distance myself from the good Irish people of Canada in the hopes of raising my stature among the general populace. I am proud of my people. I am proud of where I come from. We are here not in spite of our past, but because of it!"

The gathering cheered loudly, the type of cheers D'Arcy used to get in a time that was beginning to feel like long ago. Anglin was winning the fight—and on D'Arcy's home turf.

And the loudest cheers were coming from the very pleased Irish Society President, Bernard Devlin.

The next day, an angry D'Arcy was sitting in the Society President's office, "What's going on, Devlin? I want to hear it from your own mouth."

Devlin was uncomfortable, but proceeded gently.

"We're dropping you from the Society, D'Arcy. Timothy Anglin has been invited to join in your place."

D'Arcy nodded, then stood to leave. Devlin felt compelled to explain, "The Irish don't take kindly to your attitude lately, D'Arcy. They feel you've lost touch with their concerns for back home. We're hurting in the old country, and—"

D'Arcy interrupted with anger, "Who do you think you're talking to! Don't you think I know that? Don't you know my heart is broken and bloodied by the tragedy of our people back home? Who do you think you are, berating me about Ireland? Where were you when the men watched their children die of starvation? I was there!"

D'Arcy, who had stalked slowly toward the shaken Devlin, steadied himself, "But now I'm here. And I'll be damned before I beg for the scraps at somebody else's table again. The fight for Ireland is over. We lost! WE LOST! We can't defeat the strongest military power in the world sharing one gun between three men. Canada will belong to all of us, not a privileged few. And I can make no secret of the fact that I will fight till my dying breath so that the Irish are welcome HERE."

D'Arcy fought for breath. His hands were sweaty and shaking. His eyes were on fire.

Devlin could only add, "Good luck, D'Arcy. I'm sorry, but you're no longer welcome here."

# Chapter Fourteen

## 1865

The Boston night was wet with cold, stinging rain. In a dimly lit bar, men were getting drunk. Among them was James McGee. He was wearing his threadbare Union jacket—obviously all he owned.

The war was over for him, and his arm was heavily wrapped in old bandage rags. James was at the bottom of his emotional barrel. He was alone in a room filled with lonely men.

A fight broke out. Fights were always breaking out in drinking establishments such as this, and the authorities were slow to respond. James seemed oblivious to it.

The police did arrive eventually, and took turns harassing the drunk and broken men. When one hard, muscular man questioned James, he heard that Irish accent, and pulled him outside. James became incensed, and threw a punch. Then another. Then another.

More authorities arrived, and they turned mercilessly on the wounded soldier. He was dragged, kicked, punched, and struck with whatever the men could get their hands on.

The same night outside of Montreal was cooler, the air somehow sweeter. The metal parts of the moving train clanged and chugged its wonderful, rhythmic melody.

D'Arcy sat on one side of a four-seater car. He was facing the two strongest men in Canadian Confederation history; MacDonald, and Cartier, the man D'Arcy defeated for the Montreal West seat four years earlier and now Quebec's number one man and supporter of Confederation.

They were discussing the coming election, and the threat that Anglin was building. They all knew the newspaperman would probably win the federal seat he was running for in the New Brunswick election.

But more importantly, Anglin was slowly replacing D'Arcy as the unofficial spokesman for the country's Irish.

MacDonald said, "Already, Montreal's St. Patrick's Society has pulled its support for D'Arcy, and placed it in Anglin's camp. If we don't get him on side, we may have trouble selling Canadian unity to the Irish."

And Cartier pointed out, "Without the Irish, there will be no Confederation."

D'Arcy explained his dilemma, "Anglin's manipulating them, insisting that when I condemn the Fenians, I'm somehow condemning the Irish. He says that because of my obsession with the big picture, Canada, I've lost sight of the smaller one, the one that got me elected in the first place, the Irish community."

MacDonald and Cartier had already discussed D'Arcy's platform, and thought he should consider one of Anglin's accusations.

"You'll have to win the support of Montreal's NON-Irish community if you hope to win the election," Cartier said.

D'Arcy didn't know how to respond to this small 'betrayal', but MacDonald did.

"Men love honour," said MacDonald with a grin, "but they love winning even more."

Just then, an aid stepped up to MacDonald and handed him a message that had just come over the wire. The Prime Minister read it, then looked up with shock.

"President Lincoln's been assassinated."

D'Arcy and Mary were preparing dinner in the kitchen. She watched her pre-occupied husband as he struggled with the President's death, "The man frees the slaves, changes the way his country feels about itself, and he won't even be around to see his success played out."

Mary's face revealed something, a sense of foreshadowing. She snapped out of it, and smiled, "What do you need to wear at tomorrow's function?"

D'Arcy rolled his eyes, "A dress."

Indeed. While the Montreal Irish had been investing their money in the building of churches, the Scots had built banks. Now the men in kilts were too influential not to court.

Politics and politicians were in season, and D'Arcy played at it in various locations with equal zeal. He appeared at a succession of cultural surroundings; wearing a kilt at a Scottish dance, dipping hot, fresh maple syrup into white snow at a French sugaring-off gathering, studying a huge strudel at a German dinner, and toasting the Queen under a Union Jack.

Candelabras, hanging-lanterns, and oil floorlamps brightly lit a huge Westmount mansion. A celebration was in progress, starting with an expansive toast to a reborn political winner—D'Arcy McGee! Some of D'Arcy's more affluent supporters were throwing a celebratory masquerade party on his behalf. Everyone was in costume, and D'Arcy moved among them, leaving all laughing in his wake. These were not Montreal Irish. They were established English, Scotch, German, and French businessmen—D'Arcy's 'new' constituents. The home-owner was a transparent social-climber, and obviously saw the new Conservative as 'A' list party material. She delighted in his charm. D'Arcy knew, but was not happy knowing, that he'd won this election without the usual unanimous support of the Irish people. Cartier had told him that it was the Irishman's ability to make all Canadians feel at home that had got him re-elected.

On the street outside the huge mansion on the hill, a suspicious-looking lamplighter was doing his job.

Back inside, the rich businessman home-owner congratulated D'Arcy for his strong stand against the violent Fenians, "Ireland is lost, and we don't need another Ireland here. We need a place that's safe for all our children to prosper. A place safe for business."

The callous gentleman added, "You have children, don't you D'Arcy? A son?"

This stung. But D'Arcy swallowed his personal feelings, and offered only, "A daughter. Euphrasia."

Suddenly there was the sound of shattering glass, and someone yelled "FIRE!"

D'Arcy found Mary, and they ran out into the dark street.

There was a preliminary attempt to stop the blaze, but it soon became hopeless. The mansion burned while two dozen costumed revellers looked on. The isolated inferno could be seen for miles.

D'Arcy teased the hapless hostess, "Did you forget to invite somebody?"

A carriage arrived to take D'Arcy and his wife away just as the horse-drawn fire-engine also arrived. D'Arcy wanted to stay and help, but his driver insinuated the fire was no accident.

"I heard some people are very unhappy about you winning the election, Mr. McGee."

Mary flinched, and D'Arcy felt it. He squeezed her close, and joked reassuringly, "It's just the Irish way of saying it's official."

Mary couldn't be as glib as D'Arcy—her eyes showed her fear. He whispered to her calmly, "Don't try and hide anything behind those eyes, Mary. What is it?"

She didn't want to say, but he wouldn't let the question escape the tiny dark cabin without an answer. As tears poured down her cheeks, she said, "They'll never let you be, D'Arcy."

He looked as though he'd been slapped in the face.

She cried all the carriage-ride home, deep into the night, and into her dreams.

## Chapter Fifteen

*1867*

THE BEAUTIFUL DAY OUTSIDE THE CITY HALL MIGHT HAVE BEEN IN celebration of the Quebec Conference of 1867. Negotiations were being held around an enormous table. MacDonald from Upper Canada, Cartier from Lower Canada, the architects of Confederation, moved among the battling political representatives. Resolutions were made, and concessions were granted. Fears were assuaged with comforting guarantees. Frustrations were met with generosity.

Block by block, a new nation was being built.

D'Arcy wanted the Irish Catholics to see religious rights written into the law of this predominantly Protestant country. "I've fought my whole life for a place where the Irish could live free to practice their faith, to live fully their lives."

He explained with typical eloquence that for the Irish, Ireland was a prison, and America was a dog pound, "But

Canada is about to embrace my countrymen as equals. I want to be there when these rights are written into the document. I want to see with my own eyes FREEDOM OF RELIGION and FREEDOM OF LANGUAGE," his voice boomed out over the gathering.

Days later he stood over the draft copy of the document as a man with exceptional handwriting wrote D'Arcy's hard-won point into what would be called the British North American Act.

Done, D'Arcy glanced over at MacDonald, and smiled.

Some political concessions had been larger than others, and not all in attendance were entirely happy. But MacDonald was very pleased.

He announced that the deed was done, and stood to speak.

"With the permission of everyone present, I invite the new provinces of New Brunswick and Nova Scotia to hold their first Federal Elections, and send Members to Ottawa to serve their constituents immediately."

He then invited everyone to join him the first day of July, 1867 in Charlottetown. This would give parliament a few more months to work out constitutional details.

"We will then sign the official documents making Canada the newest nation in a rapidly changing world," the Prime Minister finished with flourish. He glanced at D'Arcy who shook his fist in enthusiastic approval.


A group of men were lead in leg chains into a large penitentiary in rural Massachusetts. Prisoners were then gathered in a holding area. They were in various stages of disarray, scattered around the large, sawdust-filled room.

One especially large, dangerous looking prisoner made his way through the crowd. He stopped when he reached another prisoner who lay sprawled on the ground.

"You're in my spot."

Without argument the weary prisoner got up to move, but the tough guy decided he wasn't satisfied.

"I want your Union jacket."

But the jacket was all that James McGee owned.

"You're going to have to earn it," James said hoarsely.

He had no money, no pride, no future—just a severely beaten face with one eye huge and closed. Without his clothes, James felt he would be nothing more than an animal.

The tough guy hit him, hard, and James fell. But he got up and repeated the message, "Going to have to do better than that."

The thug pulled a knife, "That jacket's going to cost you your life."

Suddenly, a hand grabbed the tough guy's shoulder. He spun with confidence—but then his expression changed dramatically. The thug backed down so quickly, others looked on with surprise.

James' saviour was the Confederate soldier who's life he'd saved in the Louisiana bayou, "My name is Kieron Donovan. Told you we'd meet again."

James looked at the man through his one good eye, "You said it'd be in hell."

"Was I wrong?"

James didn't think so. Then, "Who do you know Donovan? Who do you know could scare a gorilla like that?"

James was right. Donovan DID have protection. Donovan hissed so no one else could hear, "When we get out of this section, I got some people you're going to want to talk to."

Anglin was now sitting in the House of Commons, the cocky new Member from New Brunswick. He stood with confidence, and launched into an aggressive attack against the 'vile and infamous means' by which the Federalists had succeeded in New Brunswick, "The document is flawed, and unflattering to my province!"

Anglin was doing his best to undermine Confederation. But it was when he made specific reference to the 'underhanded' methods of the Member from Montreal West that D'Arcy stood to address the room, and his new Irish nemesis, "Patience sir, we're building a country."

The room laughed. Then, D'Arcy went on the attack.

"Does any Honourable Member seriously think that any treaty in the world ever gave full and entire satisfaction on every point, to every party? Does he seriously expect to have a constitutional act framed to his order or my order, or any one man's order? After all this labour and self-sacrifice, are we weak and wicked enough to alter a solemn agreement with the other provinces the moment their representatives turn their backs and go home?"

Anglin made a move to stand and challenge further, but D'Arcy's voice boomed out in finish, "We are bound sir, in honour and in good faith to carry out the measure of Union agreed upon—to promote internal peace and external security, and call into action a genuine, enduring, and heroic patriotism!"

The room erupted in enthusiastic cheers.

D'Arcy, staring hard at his Irish opponent, sat slowly. Anglin's lesson was transparent to everyone in the chamber; caught off guard, D'Arcy made a formidable opponent.

Prepared, his weapons were legion.

A voice from the backbenches chided loudly, "Welcome to Ottawa!" drawing laughter from other Members.

It was MacDonald's turn to gesture his satisfaction with D'Arcy, and he did by leading the applause.

It was night before the Members left the House. When the Prime Minister passed Anglin, he leaned over and jibed, "You should know better than to challenge McGee in front of everyone like that. The man's a statesman."

Anglin, staring at D'Arcy in the distance, said, "You see a statesman Mr. Prime Minister, but his enemies see an opportunist—a traitor."

"Perhaps because they see through the altered lenses supplied by the Member from New Brunswick?"

Turning to face Macdonald, Anglin warned, "McGee's a loose cannon. Careful next time he goes off he doesn't sink you all."

MacDonald studied Anglin for a moment, then walked off into the Ottawa night.

Reminiscent of that secret room where D'Arcy first met the violent Irish society, James now found himself surrounded by a half-dozen whispering men in a small dark prison cell. They weren't wearing torn cloth hoods, but what they did wear was somehow more frightening—the expressions of utterly desperate men, men with nothing left in the world to lose.

Their leader was an old friend of James'—D'Arcy's former editor back in Ireland, John Mitchel!

"Long time no see, McGee."

James didn't know if his life was in danger, or not—he hadn't left the Fenians on the best of circumstances.

But Mitchel hoped to regain James' support for the 'new' Fenian movement—the new, North American one.

"The Civil War is over," Mitchel said, "but it's believed that many of the former generals still lead armies—armies of discontented Irishmen. If they were to organize, they would be the most powerful army in the New World. They must do that one thing the movement has always failed to do in the past," Mitchel said, and the others waited in thick silence.

"Organize its strength."

As Mitchel continued, Donovan started pressuring James to commit to the movement, to "Take the pledge, sign the oath."

James moved to speak, squinting from the pain, "We'll all be out of here eventually."

"Then what?" Donovan pushed, "Look at yourself, McGee."

James looked at him through his battered face.

"If you ain't a Fenian," whispered Donovan, "you ain't a bloody thing."


It was in the back room of the Charlottetown Conference Hall that the last sharp edges of a newly constructed country were being smoothed out. Small political fires flamed up all over, and D'Arcy called upon his enormous charm and eloquence to put them out.

"It'll never be solved! Not now, not ever!" wailed a voice drenched with weary frustration.

D'Arcy stood apart from one Member and addressed the gathering, "If I may quote my mother, gentlemen, God Bless her Irish soul," and there was the tinkle of relaxed laughter, "whether you believe you can, or you can't—you're right."

They stared at D'Arcy in momentary silence. Then, one by one, the voices rejoined the challenge, louder and louder, soaked now with tolerance and conviction.

Soon after, with a simple exchange of handshakes, the deal was done.

A scroll was placed on a desk, and one by one the gentlemen signed it. The Prime Minister watched proudly, then leaned over to his old friend D'Arcy, and smiled, "Now you have your country."

They embraced.

John A. MacDonald reached into his coat pocket and pulled out a pen. He handed it to D'Arcy.

D'Arcy dipped the pen into the ink well, then paused. The moment was beyond the forty-three-year-old Irishman's greatest expectations, and he suddenly couldn't hide the enormity of the event from himself. No one saw his black eyes fill with tears.

And as Thomas D'Arcy McGee signed his name to the document, a teardrop fell on the signature. He stopped to wipe his eyes.

The Prime Minister was suddenly crouched beside him, tenderness in his voice, "Political exile to nation builder."

D'Arcy smiled, and said softly, "Exiled in paradise." Then he once more struggled with tears, "I've come a long way, Mr. Prime Minister."

John A. MacDonald put his hand on his shoulder, "And brought us with you."

D'Arcy raised the quill to complete his signature. The ink ran through the tear stain.


At the same time in a darker, far crueller world, a drop of blood splashed against white parchment paper. A quill was offered, and a shaking hand accepted it.

Sweat poured across the face of James McGee, and blood dripped from an awkward cut on his hand. He paused only an instant, then signed in his own blood another kind of document—the secret Fenian oath. An oath that would soon call for the overrun of the new nation to the north.


Thirty-eight men stepped out from the back room at the Charlottetown Conference Hall. They all took positions around a huge table. Some sat, some stood. A few smiled. Others were lost in private thought. For the moment all else was forgotten.

A photographer balanced the room and its gathering of egos so effortlessly, D'Arcy made a comment about how they could've used his talents in the back room.

Before anyone could laugh a huge flash bulb exploded, freezing the moment for eternity in black and white.

These proud, august men were the Fathers of Confederation.

The world returned to colour as the men came back to animated life, a symphony of congratulations, embraces, and handshakes. D'Arcy McGee stood in the eye of this joyous storm, and he couldn't stop smiling. And crying.

To himself, with pride, D'Arcy sputtered, "Mother dear, if you could see me now."

Back in the House of Commons, Prime Minister John A. MacDonald stood, "I'd like to officially welcome the newest Members from Nova Scotia and New Brunswick, and thank them for their exhaustive efforts together in forging this new country, Canada."

Then D'Arcy stood to make one comment, filling the room with soaring pride, "Today, I am—we ALL are—thoroughly and emphatically, Canadian."

The room exploded with cheers. D'Arcy, grinning like a mad fool, looked up at the Visitors Gallery. Standing among the cheering guests were Mary, and ten-year-old Euphrasia. The green-eyed daughter knew nothing of pride of country, had never seen Ireland, and politics were never discussed at home in front of her. But still her father's speech had moved her to tears.

Ex-Union and Confederate soldiers, still in various stages of tattered battle dress, were setting up shooting practice in a New England field. These were some of the new 'recruits' to the Fenian cause. This gathering of heavily armed men were preparing for war. Huge watermelons were set up as targets, balanced along a distant wooden fence. The soldiers knew how to use their rifles, and were coaching the eager recruits. Some were still teenagers.

All were Irish.

Among the ex-Union teachers was James McGee. His recruit was a terrible shot. He fired his gun, and took a chunk of wood off the fence. James told him how to adjust his shot because, "No rifle is accurate, and none is the same, so you've got to adjust to its individual flaws."

But the recruit was hopeless. They shot from a closer position, but he still missed. Closer—he missed again.

Mitchel suddenly pulled James away from his inept pupil, and whispered urgently that news had made its way from Fenian headquarters in New York. He was almost spitting with hushed excitement, "All the leftover soldiers, all the dissatisfied Irish, everyone who hated the British and all their colonies, will be joining forces with the Fenians to attack Canada!"

James was shocked. This had special impact on him, of course—and Mitchel knew it. He stared deep into James' eyes, "This is your brother's last chance. If he isn't one of us, he's one of them."

James nodded in stunned silence.

James walked shakily away from Mitchel, and returned to his pupil, "I've got to leave. You keep practising."

The recruit said no problem, then darkly, "I know what I have to do."

The tone stopped James in his tracks. He looked at the recruit with curiosity, "What's your name?"

The recruit straightened up with some pride, "James Patrick Whelan, sir."

James McGee managed a little grin, "Keep practising, Mr. Whelan." Then James moved quickly away.

Young Whelan watched him for a long moment. Then, under his breath, he said... "Bang."

Grinning, James Patrick Whelan walked right up to the watermelon, and stared at it. Then he lifted his rifle, placed it against the melon, and fired into it.

It exploded into nothing but spray.

It was late night when the front door opened to the McGee home, revealing Mary. She smiled hugely, "Thanks for coming, James."

A huge fire burned in the large fireplace. Sitting on either side of the fireplace were D'Arcy and his brother. There was a kind of cautious fencing going on between these two who loved each other very much.

D'Arcy leaned forward to light James' cigar, "Been a few years James, and you seem to be wearing all of them."

"The older you get, the better you USED to look, big brother."

Mary did what she always did when the brothers started quipping—she let them be. What she didn't know was what had been obvious to D'Arcy. James was there to deliver a warning.

"What aren't we talking about, James?"

James lifted his eyebrows, and cleared his throat, "There are people, bad people, who want to see you dead for your...beliefs."

D'Arcy laughed, startling his brother, "That's an old threat, one that was going around years ago."

James spoke with more urgency, "It's true, Darce. And that's not all of it. The whole country is threatened."

D'Arcy laughed harder, "Talk about delusions of grandeur! A gang of thieves and muggers are going to attack Canada?"

James stood, very serious, "You've become dangerously out of touch with the strength of the Irish movement. You've even lost interest in what they see when they look at you."

"What do they see James, tell me."

"I'll tell you—they see a knight in service to a British king.

A traitor. My God Darce, listen to you—you're even losing your Irish accent!"

D'Arcy stood, a feeble attempt at humour revealing the true pain in his voice, "If I ever lose my brogue, shoot me."

"When I'm gone, there'll be no one left to protect you from them, Darce."

"I don't need your kind of protection."

James spun on D'Arcy, grabbing him roughly by the collar, "D'Arcy, listen to me! If I die before you, you'd better make your peace with God."

Before the shocked D'Arcy could respond, he noticed the equally surprised Mary at the door. Embarrassed, James released D'Arcy's collar.

"I'm sorry, Mary. I'd better go."

"Don't, James, not on my account," Mary said.

But James made his way past her and toward the door. D'Arcy chased him, "James, stay here with us. I can get you work, maybe for the Canadian government."

James turned, and faced his brother with a smile, "I was born an Irishman, big brother—and I'm going to die an Irishman."

With that he took Mary in his arms, and hugged her. Then he looked into her sad, worried eyes, and smiled, "Don't fret Mary, there was never any stopping us. What was it mother used to say about her fighting sons, Darce—What's a woman to do when angels can't agree?"

He kissed her cheek, took one last look at D'Arcy, then stepped out of the house and into the chilly, starless night.

Mary stepped up to D'Arcy, and held him gently. Staring helplessly out after James, he said softly, "I'll never see him again, will I Mary?"

Later that same night in a Montreal bar, James talked to Fenians, hoping to gather support for the uprising.

"D'Arcy McGee is drunk in his affection for this place, but ours is the only policy that can right the wrongs of Ireland," he said.

One truly drunken man turned to James and stated with simple, easy cruelty, "That brother of yours will have to die if the attack succeeds."

James grabbed him roughly, "No, my friend—not as long as I'm alive."

A week later in a Parliament conference room MacDonald was in a meeting with advisers who were heatedly discussing the way Cabinet posts would be divided up. It was quickly agreed that all segments of the new country would be represented in Canada's first government. In Quebec, a problem quickly arose.

There were only two Cabinet seats in the province, and four factors had to be represented by them; French, English, Catholic, Protestant. Demographics being what they were, the two individuals would obviously have to be a French Catholic, and an English Protestant.

D'Arcy McGee, an English Catholic, was neither.

MacDonald saw he had no escape from the obvious. Incredibly, the most eloquent defender of Confederation would not reap the most obvious reward for his efforts. D'Arcy would have to be demoted from his current Cabinet post to that of an unsalaried Member of Parliament.s

While his advisers moved on to the next item of business, MacDonald remained greatly affected by what he had to do. He leaned over to a young page and whispered, "Get me D'Arcy McGee."

The Prime Minister walked with D'Arcy through the halls of government. After hearing MacDonald's piece, D'Arcy stopped, and hung his head. He turned from the Prime Minister, and began to walk slowly away. The news was devastating for the man.

MacDonald, humiliated, could only call out, "I can survive without your respect D'Arcy, but the country can't."

D'Arcy stopped again, turned, and said softly, "You may not survive at all unless you tell your Montreal garrison to stand ready."

He turned, and walked slowly away.

MacDonald watched, a thousand emotions on his face. Then, to himself, "Don't quit on me D'Arcy. Not now."

Mary McGee stepped out of a St. Catherine's Street food store, and walked down the street with Euphrasia in tow. She made her way through a thick crowd of people, and those who recognized her wished her husband well. But then the sound of one man's voice stopped her cold, "Your husband's going to die for his beliefs."

Mary spun around, but couldn't see who had spoken to her. She bundled Euphrasia close, and moved quickly away.

Mary kissed her daughter goodnight, and tucked her into bed. She heard a noise, and startled, turned. D'Arcy was standing at the doorway, watching his wife labour over the youngster.

Concerned about his family's welfare, Mary reassured D'Arcy they need not worry, "You're an excellent lawyer, and we'll get by with the money you make at that."

She held him tight, and whispered, "We have control of our own destiny. No one to answer to but ourselves. What else can happen?"

It was June of 1866 when one thousand American Irish under the command of Col. O'Neill, a man who had fought under Sherman, turned their weapons on Canada. Some of those Fenians washed up on the St. Lawrence shoreline and prepared to attack Montreal. They'd come across the river under cover of night, boat loads of the Irish Brigade—motley leftovers from the victorious Union Army, and the defeated Confederates.

They were heavily armed, carrying weapons not only for themselves, but also for the Canadian Irish the Fenians expected would rise with them to destroy this Canadian arm of the British Empire.

They hoped to become an attacking force of thousands.

One platoon of twenty-four men was being led by a vicious, demanding taskmaster—D'Arcy's brother, James McGee.


A soldier of the Montreal Garrison ran in and announced that the Fenians had landed on the riverfront. In fact, the attacking force from America extended from Ottawa all the way to New Brunswick. But considering the extent of the attack, the force was thin—no more than a few hundred heavily-armed former soldiers were moving on Montreal.

The garrison commander moved quickly to rally his troops, "You know what to do."

Indeed, because of D'Arcy's advance warnings to the soldiers, they had been expecting the attack, and were in fact prepared for much worse than the Fenians managed to muster on this day.


Incredibly, Fenians were walking up the dark, abandoned streets and shouting for the Irish to wake up, accept their weapons and join the attack. They were loud, arrogant, confident—firing their guns into the night.

James McGee, filled with confused, misguided hatred, yelled curses against the British Empire, "No more secrets—we are on the streets of your city!" It was one bright moment of glory for the violent movement.

But no one was responding. The streets stayed empty. The Irish of Montreal did not want to join. They simply closed their windows and their doors.

The Fenians DID get one huge response, but not the one they'd hoped for. The Montreal garrison was coming after them, and they meant business. The Fenians scattered, and most ran back to the St. Lawrence and their boats.

The moment had been like a flame burning brightest before it went out. As quickly as it began, the fight seemed to be over.

One Fenian yelled at James, "They won't budge! Your damned brother's turned the Irish against us!"

James McGee was taken aback by the charge, but shouted at his comrades to fight on, "I'll shoot any man that turns his back on me!"

But they peeled away one by one until he was left to fight alone. One lone voice called back in the dark, "He won't have you protecting him forever, McGee!"

Fenians scrambled for escape, some throwing themselves into the St. Lawrence and swimming frantically across. All of them threw down their weapons, either along the shore or into the river.

James crashed into the same bar he'd visited months before, and was met by a dozen cowering patrons. He threw an extra rifle at the man who earlier had threatened to kill his brother, "I'm giving you permission to fight for your beliefs."

"This is our last chance!" he shouted.

No one moved.

"Don't tell me you'll live under British rule! Do you want Ireland all over again!"

Nothing. Just a room filled with silence and darkness.

"Well, God save the Irish from themselves," James said, his voice breaking. Then he was gone.

James burst out onto the street—and found himself face to face with a platoon of Redcoats.

"Bastards!"

He raised his rifle, but was hit immediately by a hail of bullets, and dropped to the ground. He tried to get up, but no part of his body could hear his commands.

His eyes fell on a house across the street. His brother's house. The view was slowly erased by his own blood as it spilled across his eyes. With his last breath, he whispered, "D'Arcy...what have you done to us?"

Then, alone among enemies, James McGee died.

At the Montreal Morgue, Mary McGee was being led by a family friend to a room filled with the dead bodies of fallen Fenians.

"That's him," she said, a tremble in her voice, "that's James McGee." She would never forgive herself for having expected to find her troubled brother-in-law there.

A late-night emergency session concerning the Fenian attack was coming to an end in the House of Commons. Word had reached the Prime Minister from the American President that the attack on Canadian borders had not been condoned by the government. It was an isolated act, and the American government had already moved to make sure it wouldn't happen again.

Timothy Anglin, Member from New Brunswick, stood and suggested that the Fenians received no support in Canada because of the hard work of D'Arcy McGee, "The Irish-Canadian has made no secret of his distaste for the Fenians, and his influence perhaps has never been as evident."

The Prime Minister agreed, and the House thanked D'Arcy with warm applause.

D'Arcy looked across the room at his Irish opponent. The New Brunswicker smiled back.

Later, when members were filing out of the huge room, D'Arcy was stopped in his seat by a page who handed him an envelope. It was a telegram from Mary.

D'Arcy sat back as he read. In moments he was alone in the huge room. No one was left to hear his heart break.

D'Arcy stood, staring around the chamber in disbelief. Then he crushed the letter in his hands, overwhelmed with emotional pain. He slammed his fists against his desk, and began to scream up at the gods... "NO NO NO NO NO!!!!!"

D'Arcy stumbled out into the centre of the great room, and collapsed to the floor. Pages responding to the shouts entered the room, and ran over to his aid.

Back home in Montreal, D'Arcy was in St. Patrick's Cathedral taking confession with his parish priest. D'Arcy, seated, could say nothing. He was crying. Finally, he managed to mutter... "I murdered my brother."

D'Arcy walked down the stairs outside the Cathedral when the priest stepped out of the huge doors behind him, "D'Arcy?"

The distraught D'Arcy stopped, but didn't turn around. The priest came down the stairs toward him. Face to face, the priest took D'Arcy in his arms, and both men cried.

# Chapter Sixteen

The door to the Boston bar was locked, and only very specific patrons were being allowed in. There was loud, raucous drinking. One man stood and shouted, "McGee called the Fenians animals in Canadian Parliament today. He said only wild animals must die from violence. Well I say that wild animals also die from starvation! And given the choice—I'll die fighting to feed my family than have them starve in another potato famine!"

Angry, vulgar cheers went up.

"He said Irish questions and Canadian politics don't mix!"

A round of beer was brought to a table, and another man stood with his glass held high, "Quiet! Everyone! A toast, to all friends of Ireland!"

They lifted their glasses and mugs, and the toast continued... "And to the man who kills Thomas D'Arcy McGee!"

A huge cheer went up, and everyone drank deeply.

Even as they barked and shouted they knew the boisterous moment would pass into hangover, and nothing would come of it.

Except for one man who sat and stared out from his own dark, troubled silence. It was a young, well-dressed tailor named James Patrick Whelan—James McGee's pupil at the Fenian training camp.

The one who was a terrible shot.


Mary and D'Arcy were sitting in front of their fireplace. D'Arcy had said that he was considering dropping out of politics, and building up his law practice. Mary didn't know how to respond—her husband was in unassuagable emotional pain.

"Could be my time as a politician has passed. Political fortunes rise and fall, and my time may come again, but for now I'm seriously considering changing hats," he looked at her and smiled a small, sad smile, "find a place where I feel more needed."

He was lying to her, to himself, covering up. Mary held him, "D'Arcy, I don't know what you want to hear."

What they both heard was a knock at the front door.

Mary opened it and found the Prime Minister standing there.

"Hello, Mary."

He was somewhat humiliated to see Mrs. McGee, considering his professional treatment of her husband, but she was bright, "D'Arcy will be happy to see you, John."

MacDonald signalled the driver of a huge black carriage, and stepped into the house. The Prime Minister joined the McGees in front of the fire, and got quickly to the point, "D'Arcy, I need your help in Ottawa."

Almost startled, the McGees glanced at each other.

MacDonald, very concerned, continued, "Nova Scotia has elected Canada's first provincial separatist government, and intends to scuttle the newly created Dominion if new demands aren't met."

Mary watched as D'Arcy moved subtly forward in his chair, his interest obvious.

MacDonald saw it, too, "I'm certain the General Parliament won't carry any concessions, or give any advantages to Nova Scotia. Great Britain has interfered, calling a conference in London to discuss the constitutional crisis. Nova Scotia has sent Joseph Howe, leader of the new provincial party. We've sent a capable man, Sir Charles Tupper, Nova Scotia member of federal parliament."

"We need someone to defend my government's policies in the House," the Prime Minister added.

"Why me?"

"Because you are the voice of Confederation, D'Arcy. And history will remember you that way."

Considering the Prime Minister's recent exclusion of D'Arcy from his Cabinet, MacDonald was uncomfortable with the request, and D'Arcy saw this. The Prime Minister couldn't look D'Arcy in the eye when he reminded him of the Irishman's unwavering loyalty in the past.

Mary glanced at her husband, and suddenly laughed. When both men look at her strangely, she looked at the Prime Minister with mock surprise, "I'm sorry. I assumed you were joking."

D'Arcy tried to stop her, "Mary—"

Her anger boiled over, "Is this what they mean by delegating responsibility, D'Arcy? His 'new' Cabinet can't take the heat, so he wants to throw someone expendable in front of the fire?"

D'Arcy had NEVER seen her like this, "Mary?"

"Look what happened to President Lincoln! Some lunatic tripped history as it passed just to become a part of it!"

D'Arcy stood, "Mary! He's the Prime Minister."

Standing, she shouted, "And you're my husband!" Then she faced MacDonald, "If you didn't want my opinion, you shouldn't have come into my home asking for it."

With that, she stormed out of the room. D'Arcy followed, "Mary, wait."

He caught up to her in the hallway and held her, talking softly, "Mary, in these last few years I've lost a son, a brother, and the means to support myself. I don't want to lose this country."

She looked into his face, searching for the truth in his eyes, "Do you really want to do this all again?"

They both knew what this question meant—if D'Arcy returned to his volatile public persona, he might attract the kind of attention his brother James had warned him about.

"Mary, more than anything."


D'Arcy watched MacDonald climb into his carriage. The Prime Minister looked back with genuine sincerity, "Thank you, D'Arcy."

D'Arcy sighed, grinned, "Old Irish saying—Dance with the one who brung ya."

"Sorry about Mary. I realize she's got reason to be concerned about this Fenian business."

D'Arcy laughed, "Not like us, eh Prime Minister?"

"Not worried at all."

"If the Fenians get me, I promise not to leave this mortal coil until we have that drink."

MacDonald smiled.

"You WILL have a drink with me, won't you, John?"

"You're the one won't drink with me, D'Arcy." Then the Prime Minister shook his head, grinned, and signalled his driver.

Hours later, as they drifted off to sleep, Mary's whisper went a long way toward explaining her behaviour, "We're going to have another child, D'Arcy."


D'Arcy and Mary were skating on the beautiful ice of Beaver Lake. A million miles away, bright stars were blinking. Oil lanterns swung from the bare branches of the trees that lined the man-made pond nestled atop Mt. Royal, casting a flickering glow on everything. Only courting couples were left on the ice. The area was almost surreal, dream-like for its utter romantic beauty. But this was, after all, Canada in winter.

Mary leaned close and told D'Arcy something her father once told her, a long time ago. "You can count the days of your life that are truly happy on the fingers of one hand."

D'Arcy, "Is this one of those days, Mary?"

She looked into his eyes, and the words came out in ghosts of frosty air, "This has been all of those days."

D'Arcy's expression changed, and he kissed her. Nothing was said, but D'Arcy and Mary were sharing the same fear—that D'Arcy would not be alive much longer.

When he finally spoke, he couldn't look her in the eyes, "I haven't paid enough attention to you, have I Mary? I'm sorry. You know if I could now, I—"

But Mary interrupted, "You wouldn't change a thing," she offered softly, "and neither would I."

She grinned, and skated away, "How many women can say their husband was late for dinner for five straight years because he was building a country?"

D'Arcy's eyes filled with joy over this simple fact, "Mary, I've helped build something that can't be burned down with a single match."

Mary agreed, and held her husband close, "Canada will be here for a million years."

She smiled at him with much love, and he smiled back. Then, suddenly, D'Arcy began to cry.

"What's wrong D'Arcy, why are you crying?"

He held her there, as other skaters passed, staring through the tears on his face, "From that moment I first saw you Mary, working the printing press—you've always been too beautiful for my eyes."

Neither knew that still tangled in the bare wintry branches of a maple tree on the edge of the pond was Patrick's long lost puppet. The brightly painted face had long ago faded into the cloth, and the cloth had long ago faded into wispy rags and feathery ribbons. But ten years of summer rains and winter snow had not been able to dislodge the object of so much love from its place.

Nothing ever would.

D'Arcy was sound asleep in his bed, facing away. A hand reached over to stroke his brow. Mary was lying beside him, very awake. As she touched his unhandsome face, she sang softly his mother's song, "The Wearing of the Green."

She finished a few lines, then leaned closer to whisper into his dreams, "I will love you till the day I die."

D'Arcy was also very much awake, and his eyes were wet with tears. The next day he would be heading back to Ottawa.

They had found their own way not to say goodbye.

The next morning, D'Arcy was gone. Mary held baby Agnes in her arms and read aloud a poem her husband had left by the bed. Wee Agnes cooed with satisfaction as her mother spoke the melody of words:

> "I dreamed a dream when the woods were green,
> And my April heart made an April scene,
> In the far, far distant land,
> That even I might something do
> That would keep my memory for the true,
> And my name from the spoiler's hand!"

Mary's hand went to cover her trembling mouth, and she fought the tears back. Then she realized that baby Agnes was staring at her. She touched her child's face reassuringly, "Your father needn't worry Agnes. He'll be twice remembered, because Canadians will never forget their first politicians. And the Irish never forget their poets."

Agnes, satisfied, returned to the mystery of her toes, and Mary's thoughts returned to her husband. An unhandsome man, whose smile alone could lift her heart out from the darkest places. Not a large man, whose dreams alone could lift a country out of the wilderness.

Up in the House of Commons gallery was sitting James Patrick Whelan, the Fenian with the lousy shot. He looked as frightening now as he had looked inept then. And he never took his eyes off of the Member from Montreal West, Thomas D'Arcy McGee.

Down below, another drama was unfolding. Bridges, a Member from Nova Scotia, was making unsettling comments about the new Union. As MacDonald had warned D'Arcy, Nova Scotia had just nominated Canada's first provincial separatist party, hell-bent on pulling out of the constitution virtually before the country had even begun.

This was D'Arcy's cue, and he stood that day to make a speech that his country would never forget...

> *"We live in a world flush with immigrants looking for a better life, and a dozen nations do battle over these precious settlers. Our New Nation lacks the golden rivers of California, and the luxurious climate of Australia. Indeed, most immigrants are greeted in our land under a wreath of Canadian snow.*

*So, what can we nation builders give Canada that will render her land habitable to all persons? We can give each individual their fairly-won place in her history.*
*What can we guarantee our new immigrants?*
*Try justice!*
*Try conciliation!*
*Try equality!*

*We cannot convince anyone we have built a home the envy of the free world when it is filled with trap doors, escape hatches and secret corridors. The world will not commit to a country that will not commit to itself.*

*Our Canada is not a country that will burn brightly for a short time, but a country that has been designed to burn steadily...*

*...Once, and for all."*

D'Arcy McGee suddenly caught a sob, then continued in a barely controlled voice...

*"Little do they know who have never felt it themselves, how sad a burden is hopeless love of country. With great pride I tell you that I was born an Irishman. But with my last breath I swear to you, I will die a Canadian!"*

He stood there, his entire body trembling with passion he could barely comprehend. There was not a sound in the House. Just a mass holding of breath.

There was Bridges, whose own comments had provoked the speech, staring in stunned silence.

Anglin, struggling with emotion, his eyes wet.

Cartier, his head bowed.

And Prime Minister MacDonald, with his eyes bright, filled with pride, raising a fist into the air, "Here Here!"

The House followed MacDonald's lead, and exploded into genuine shouts and applause of gratitude.

D'Arcy looked around, startled. Confused, he fell back into his seat, as if he didn't know the outpouring of emotion was for him.

Finally, he smiled an embarrassed smile.

It was after midnight when D'Arcy was walking alone down the dark Ottawa street and a young government page called out to him, "I thought we'd be there all night."

D'Arcy smiled, "Would've been symbolic after a night such as this, don't you think—watching the sun come up on Canada?"

The page waved, and trotted on.

D'Arcy turned up the street he lived on, and heard the scuffling of footsteps behind him. He stopped, turned.

"Who goes there?"

The air was cold, and his breath escaped in tiny ghosts. But not a sound came back.

D'Arcy shrugged it off and turned up the steps to his Ottawa residence. He stopped at the front door and foraged around in his pocket, producing a key. He stuck the key in the door—

—When the ghost of someone else's cold breath suddenly wafted up against his face.

In an instant, he knew.

"Mary."

A gun went off, a loud BANG, and D'Arcy collapsed to the icy pavement, a small trickle of blood staining the white snow around his head. The assassin ran off into the cold night.

D'Arcy whispered through a final cloud of frosty breath, "James, what have you done to us."

A voice rang out, "He's been shot! D'Arcy McGee's been shot!"

The shouts attracted the attention of John A. MacDonald, who was also just leaving the late night session, and he came running. He fell to his knees, wiping the bloody snow away from his friend's collar, and from his face.

"D'Arcy? D'Arcy?!"

McGee's eyes opened. It took a moment for the fatally wounded Irishman to recognize MacDonald. His lips moved, but no words came out.

MacDonald whispered emotionally, "You promised me a drink before you go, old friend."

D'Arcy's eyes softened, then closed, a tear running back into his unruly hair. MacDonald could do nothing but watch as D'Arcy died in his arms.

Then the Prime Minister of Canada picked Thomas D'Arcy McGee up in his arms, and carried him into the house.

The assassin's gun was left still smoking in the snow by the door.

It was a beautiful late summer day when Prime Minister John A. MacDonald walked along the forest of tombs in Montreal's sprawling Cote des Neiges Cemetery. As he did, he recalled his own voice from a speech he'd delivered in the House of Commons, addressing the Members as well as the nation with this final soliloquy—

*"How could he have known that his key was not unlocking the doorway to his home, but the gates of heaven. Now the brain then teeming with thought, richly stored with learning, and quickened with a genius rarely surpassed, is at rest, and*

the tongue, so eloquent, is silenced forever. And on this sad day we know we are one nation, with one heart, because it is broken."

He turned up a path, and walked passed a row of majestic burial chambers.

"Now he is in the care of our memories. May his death on behalf of his country serve to give strength to our hearts to do or die, if necessary in her cause; and as we are all united here today around the memory of Thomas D'Arcy McGee, may we become more united in brotherly feeling and holy charity, all animated with his spirit, all labouring for the same great ends—

The Prime Minister stopped, and took a deep breath. He was standing in front of D'Arcy McGee's crypt.

*The crypt of Thomas D'Arcy McGee*

*—and then from those ashes a new country shall spring, and with his blood shall be watered and fostered the young tree of our national greatness."*

The sound of thunderous applause slowly receded back into his thoughts, and the music of birds and rustling trees took over.

MacDonald placed a huge bouquet of flowers outside the crypt door, his bottom lip trembling.

"You encouraged your country's builders to aim for the moon, D'Arcy. But it is you who has fallen among the stars."

John A. MacDonald pulled a flask out from inside his coat, and raised it to his fallen friend.

"Thanks for waiting, D'Arcy."

Then he took a long, deep drink. His eyes closed for a long moment, savouring the whiskey, and trying to hold on to a memory already slipping away.

"'Til we meet again, old friend," said MacDonald. Then he placed the flask at the foot of the vault door, turned away, and soon disappeared up the winding path.

Then, from somewhere lost in the tangled webs of time and place, D'Arcy's mother called out, "D'Arcy? D'Arcy?"

Because it was 1831 again, and young D'Arcy was hiding in the tall grass of an Irish field on the shores of Carlingford Lough. He'd found the huge gun at his tiny feet, picked it up, studied it, and thrown it away.

He jumped up, and ran straight into his brother. They leapt about and hugged each other joyously. Then they bolted together after their mother, and a remarkable life.

# Addendum

Mary McGee died only three years after her husband and the only home they ever owned, on St. Catherine's Street in Montreal, was broken up. The McGees of Ireland were survived by two daughters—Euphrasia ended up in Oakland, California, while Agnes stayed in Montreal.

At the time of this book's publication in 1996, the country of Canada, for the third time in four years, had been selected by the United Nations as the best country in the world to live in.

To fall among the stars, indeed.

# Bibliography

*Thomas D'Arcy McGee;* by Alexander Brady; Toronto; The Macmillan Company of Canada Limited; 1925

*The Life and Speeches of Hon. George Brown;* by Alex Mackenzie; Toronto; The Globe Printing Company; 1882

*Brown of the Globe;* by J.M.S. Careless; Toronto; The Macmillan Company of Canada Limited; 1963

*Thomas D'Arcy McGee, Visionary of the Welfare State in Canada;* by Bill Kirwin; The University of Calgary Faculty of Social Welfare; 1981

*A History of Canada;* W.L. Morton, Executive Editor; The Canadian Publishers; McClelland and Stewart Limited; 1964

*1825 – D'Arcy McGee – 1925, A Collection of Speeches and Addresses;* by The Honourable Charles Murphy, K.C., LL.D.; Toronto; The Macmillan Company of Canada Limited, at St. Martin's House; 1937

Michael Leo Donovan

*The Critical Years; The Union of British North America 1857-1873;* The Canadian Centenary Series; McClelland and Stewart Limited

*Hon. Thos. D'Arcy McGee, A Sketch of His Life and Death;* by Fennings Taylor; John Lovel, St. Nicholas Street; 1868

*The Ardent Exile;* by Josephine Phelan; Toronto; The Macmillan Company of Canada Limited; 1951

*The Life of Thomas D'Arcy McGee;* by Isabel Skelton; Gardenvale; Garden City Press; 1925

# Thomas D'Arcy McGee

To understand the impact this Irish exile had on his Canadian Countrymen may best be described by the comments delivered after his death:

*Delivered in French by Hector Fabre, Senator from Quebec:*

"As a speaker—now that he is no more, it can be said without offence to the living—he had not, he never has had, a rival; he will have no successor. No one united in such a degree the warmth of inspiration, the originality and nobleness of thought, the flow of witticisms, to a perfection of form which, rare everywhere, is unknown here."

*George Ross, Premier of Ontario, recalling from his youth a D'Arcy McGee speech on the future of Canada:*

"I have never heard or seen Mr. McGee before that day—or since. I had no preconception of oratory as a fine art or what were its essential elements. I had a vague idea, however, that there was something in it beyond the reach of ordinary mortals, which, if not exactly supernatural, had a spark of divine power or a sanctity peculiarly the gift of the gods. But whatever it was, I was there to see and learn for myself."

*Sir John A. MacDonald, Canada's first Prime Minister:*

"If ever a soldier who fell on the field of battle in the front of the fight deserved well of his country, Thomas D'Arcy McGee deserved well of Canada and its people."

*From a speech about D'Arcy McGee delivered by W.A. Foster:*

"He dared to be national in the face of provincial selfishness, and with persuasive eloquence drew us closer together as a people, pointing out to each what was good in the other—Yes, one who breathed into our New Dominion the spirit of a proud self-reliance, and first taught Canadians to respect themselves.

"He spoke, and the nation listened."